mafia boss

Syndicate of Sin

emilia rose

content warning

This book is considered a dark romance and includes brutality, murder, mention of child abuse, and other gruesome topics. If any of these things makes you uncomfortable, I suggest not reading.

1

cristian

KILLING ALWAYS CAME EASILY to me. Loving did not.

I held the muzzle of my gun right between Charlie's eyes and stared down at the guy, feeling no ounce of sympathy for such a pitiful, filthy man. He had corrupted the Ricci name by taking those children, doing things so sinful to them that he'd be sent straight to fucking hell. Right where he belonged.

"I trusted you, Charlie," I said through clenched teeth, taking the safety off. "And you did the one thing you and I both know this family *never* does." I pushed the gun further against his forehead, watching the tears fall down his cheeks. "Tell me what you did, so I know *you* know why I'm about to shoot you fucking dead."

"Please," he pleaded. "Please, Cristian ... I've known you since you were a boy." More tears slid down his cheeks, but he'd had no sympathy when he was touching those fucking children, so I had no sympathy now. "Don't do this."

I grabbed a knife from the pocket of my suit pants, opened it, and slid it right across his cheek, carving a deep gash in the thing he'd spent thousands on. When I had been young and impression-able, I'd thought it was to look good for the women. But now, I

1

knew it was to appear attractive and youthful, trusting even, to young boys.

He grasped his face and screamed. "Cristian. Please ..." Blood spewed out of his wound.

"Fucking tell me, Charlie, or I'll do it again. You don't deserve an easy fucking death."

Nothing.

I slid the knife across his other cheek, then broke his nose just for the fucking fun of it. "You're a piece of shit. If my father were still alive, he'd be fucking disgusted with himself, knowing that one of his best men did this."

Charlie grasped his nose and doubled over, spitting up blood. "I won't do it again. I swear, Cristian. You have to believe me. It was one time. One time! It didn't even mean anything. I didn't do anything to the kid."

My jaw twitched, my finger hovering over the trigger. I didn't want him to be on this fucking planet anymore, didn't care about torturing his ass. He deserved death—cold and final death—more than any of the men I had killed.

"Boss," one of my guards said. "Ben wants to see you."

Ben. I pressed my lips together at the sound of his name. Another man I'd have to get rid of soon if he continued to disappoint me. I didn't have time for his bullshit now though. I had other assholes to deal with.

"I'm busy."

Someone pushed the door open.

"Please, boss," Ben said, stepping into the room without fucking permission.

Couldn't he fucking see that I was in the middle of something important?

The guard grabbed him by the shoulder to shove him out, but I stopped him.

"He can stay," I said, gliding my tongue across the inside of my teeth.

Let him stay, so I can show him what will happen to him if he doesn't clean up his act.

Ben stared at Charlie, then at the blood on my hands. "I can come back. Sorry for—"

"Sit the fuck down," I said to Ben. "You wanted to talk to me. You interrupted me. You will wait."

Ben scrambled to a seat at my desk, and I turned back to Charlie.

"You're a sorry excuse for a Ricci," I said. "Take him to the fucking dungeon and chain him up. I'll be down to handle him later."

Two guards looped their arms around his and picked him up. Charlie tried scrambling away, shaking his head back and forth and telling me that I was making the biggest mistake of my life. After they took him out the back door, I stuffed my gun into the waistband of my pants and walked around my desk.

"Did you do as I'd asked?" I asked Ben.

Ben glanced from the back door to me and looked at his lap. "Boss, I can't do this anymore." He shook his head. "Please, I can't." That fearful expression crossed his face, the same one I'd told him he was going to have after gambling away my money.

I stared at him, my tongue gliding across my teeth again as I took a sip of my sambuca. It tasted sour in my mouth tonight, or maybe that was just the thought of a Ricci ever doing that to a child.

Music thumped from my club into my office, and I tried to use the alcohol to relax because I was one moment away from killing this fucker right here. I didn't have the patience tonight, and he was beginning to become a nuisance.

"You steal *my* money, are thousands of dollars in gambling debt, and think you can ask to just stop?" I asked, rage boiling inside of me. My jaw tightened. "You have the fucking audacity to ask me to let you go?" My voice was quiet—deathly quiet.

"Please," Ben said.

I slammed my hand on my desk. "I gave you a choice two months ago. Work for me or get a bullet straight through your head.

You chose to work for me, so that's what you're going to fucking do."

Ben shook his head. "I can't do this anymore. I can't kill people."

After blowing out a deep breath, I looked him straight in the eyes. "What happens when your fiancée finds out about your *little* problem? Huh? She doesn't know what you do, does she?" When he shook his head, I cracked a small smile. "Maybe she should find out why you've been out late for so many late nights, how you're thousands of dollars in debt, that you don't have a fucking cent to your name, and that you have an addiction you can't fucking overcome."

"Don't tell her, please," he said, shaking his head.

"I suppose she doesn't know about all the money you've taken from her too."

"I haven't taken anything from her."

Lie.

"You haven't gambled away your savings yet? What about that ring on her finger? Does she know it's fake?"

"It's not fake," Ben said, but he couldn't look me in the eye when he said it. After I let him simmer for a few moments, he shook his head. "It doesn't matter if it's fake or not. She loves me, and I love her."

I placed my gun on the desk and took another swig of my sambuca, letting it sit in my mouth for a moment as I stared at the man in front of me, who seemed to be spooked.

"Her name is Roxie, isn't it?" I asked, letting her name roll off my tongue. "She's very beautiful. It'd be quite terrible if I had to take her from you to pay off your debt."

"Please, don't. She'd leave me if she found out. She would fucking leave me."

"You want out, don't you?" I asked. "There's a price."

He stood and placed his hands on *my* desk. "Please, boss. Don't involve her. She doesn't know anything about where I've been going, what I've been doing, who I am. It would break her heart."

"You love her?" I asked, brow arched.

He nodded frantically. "More than anything. I do this all for her. Please, don't involve her in this. It's my fuckup."

I stood too, grabbed my gun, and walked around him. A bead of sweat rolled down that lousy neck of his. I should've broken it when I had the chance.

"You don't do this for her. You do this because *you* gambled away *my* money and thought you could get away with it. You don't love her because if you did, you'd have dropped her the moment you got involved with me."

"I do love her," he said, sounding so sure of it.

"You don't. You're just selfish." But so was I.

I had only seen her a handful of times in passing, but I knew she'd be mine one day.

After opening the door for him, I gestured for him to leave. "You're not out, but you're going to bring her here tomorrow night. Ten p.m. Don't be late."

I had business with another family tomorrow night about more men who'd made bad decisions involving children, but I'd be willing to make room for sweet ol' Roxie too.

2

roxie

I SIPPED on my jasmine tea and stared at the dark TV screen, trying to keep my eyes open just enough to stay awake until Ben came home. The neon green light of the clock read 3:04 a.m. It was so late—so freaking late—and I had to be up in four hours.

My eyes fluttered closed, yet I willed myself to stay awake.

Every night for the past two weeks, Ben had been coming home past midnight. And every night, I'd fall asleep before he came home because I needed to sleep for work, but not tonight. Tonight, I was going to find out where the hell he had been because this wasn't the Ben I had been dating for the past three years.

Another fifteen minutes passed, and I found myself coming in and out of sleep, accepting and rejecting the darkness that seemed to always creep up on me at this time. I had only been thinking and dreaming the worst about him lately, but maybe … maybe I was just getting cold feet before our wedding.

He had proposed a month ago, yet something felt off. And all *I* could think about was that he was getting cold feet too, that he was out, enjoying the last of his single life with another girl before he married me.

Our apartment door creaked open, and Ben stumbled into the room, trying to be as quiet as he could. But he didn't know that I had stayed awake for the first time this week. He didn't know that I was freaking determined to know where he had been.

I mumbled his name, but instead of coming into the living room to greet me, he hurried straight to the bathroom and shut the door, the smell of alcohol, covered by cheap cologne, drifting through our small apartment.

When I heard the water start, I shot up from the couch and wiped my tired eyes.

"Ben!" I shouted, knocking on the bathroom door. "Ben, we need to talk." He didn't answer, so I banged on the door with the side of my fist. "Ben, open up!"

The water hammered down on the shower walls, so I hit my fist against the door, louder and louder until it was trembling. I was thinking the absolute worst. Ben had been out with another girl, telling her things he only told me, letting her touch him … and now, he was trying to hide the evidence, cover up her perfume with my lemon-scented soap.

"Now, Ben. We need to talk. This is serious."

After waiting another two minutes, I found the key to the bathroom door hidden in the kitchen and unlocked it, stepping into the steamy room.

"Ben, we need to talk. Why are you ignoring me?" I asked.

"Go to sleep, Roxie," Ben said from inside the shower. Our shower curtain was basically hanging by a thread at this point, and the room was small enough to barely hold two people. "It's late, and you have work tomorrow morning."

His clothes were sitting in the sink, and because I knew he'd never admit to cheating on me—what guy would?—I grabbed them and hoped to find a note, to smell perfume, looking for something that would give me a clue as to where he had been these past two weeks.

But as soon as they touched my skin, I saw the blood. My fingers trembled as I unraveled them. They weren't soaked in blood, but instead splattered with it. I shook my head, my eyes wide, my heart hammering against my chest.

"What is this?" I asked, voice so quiet that I almost didn't hear myself. "Why is there blood on your shirt?"

The water shut off, and Ben stepped out of the shower, wrapping a towel around his waist. He snatched the clothes from me, jaw tight.

"I said, go to bed." He stormed out of the bathroom, tracking water all over our dingy apartment floor to the bedroom.

After thrusting the clothes into a black garbage bag and throwing it in our trash can, he rifled through his closet to find something to wear. I followed after him every step of the way.

"Why can't you tell me?" I asked. "I'm your freaking fiancée. I deserve to know."

If there was one thing I hated the most in this world, it was men who lied. He could've gotten into an accident. He could've gotten into a fight at the bar. He could've fucking killed someone, for all I knew. And I would be there for him. But I couldn't fucking deal with a liar.

"Are you cheating on me?" I asked. It didn't explain the blood, but it was the only explanation I had come up with for his sudden coldness the past two weeks. "Tell me you haven't been cheating on me."

"I haven't been cheating on you," he said, his body completely tense. "I would never cheat on you."

"Then where have you been?" I asked, staring up at the ceiling with tears in my eyes. "And why do you have blood on your clothes?"

"That's none of your business," he said to me, voice harsher than usual.

"It is my business, Ben. I'm going to marry you."

He snatched my chin in his hand and slammed me against the wall. The air left my damn throat, and I stared up at him with wide eyes, never having experienced *this* Ben. He had never laid his damn hands on me before.

"Leave it alone," he said through clenched teeth, sounding out each word as if I couldn't hear him.

After a few moments, he released my chin and took a deep breath. "I'm sorry," he whispered, walking away and shaking his head. "I'm sorry, Roxie. I didn't mean to touch you like that."

I stepped away from him when he came closer to me. I shouldn't have asked where he was. I should've just gone to fucking bed and woken up tomorrow like everything was fine. Sometimes, ignorance was fucking bliss.

Instead of prying anymore, I slid into bed, turned onto my side, and stared into the darkness. "Good night," I whispered, trying hard to keep my voice steady and unwavering.

Tears welled up in my eyes. The feeling of his hand closing around my throat so viciously like that haunted me.

The bed dipped next to me, Ben sliding under the covers with me. "I'm sorry," he whispered, fingers brushing against my hip to pull me closer.

I pushed him away. If he didn't want to tell me the truth, I didn't want him to touch me.

"I'm taking you out tomorrow night. We're going somewhere nice," he said, then turned onto his side to face the opposite direction.

I pressed my lips together and refused to make any noise, any whimper, any sign of weakness. God, I did so much for this man. I worked my ass off to get us out of debt—or at least tried to—had stayed up late with him to watch him play those stupid online card games when we started dating, spent a weekend in Vegas with him when I should've been working. And he couldn't even tell me why he had been coming home late and why there was fucking blood on his clothes.

Before I could fall asleep, the bed shook slightly, and I could hear the quiet sobs coming from his side.

"I fucked up, Roxie," he whispered so lowly, probably thinking that I had fallen asleep. "I fucked it all up."

3

roxie

SO MUCH FOR wanting to take me out somewhere nice to spend time with me.

Sure, we *might've* been at the fanciest, most upper-class club in all of Manhattan, and I *might've* been on my second glass of After-glow Elixir sweet white wine that was *way* too expensive for our budget, and some guys from across the bar *might've* been looking me up and down the entire night and making me feel good for the first time in two weeks, but Ben was nowhere to be found.

He had disappeared almost half an hour ago, telling me that he needed to use the restroom. My fingers turned white against the glass as I tried to think of the best-case scenario. Ben was just taking the biggest dump of his life—not in there, fucking some girl—while I sat here, stupidly waiting for him.

A couple of the men dressed in black stared at me from across the bar, their wandering eyes dark and sinful. I swallowed some more of my wine and pressed my knees together, knowing that I shouldn't ever feel this way about any man who wasn't my fiancé.

But he hadn't paid much attention to me since we had gotten engaged, had left me alone for weeks now, barely touching me when he got home for the night. The most I had gotten was a kiss on the forehead lately.

I tore my gaze away, heat crawling up my neck, and pushed my empty glass to the edge of the counter. Fuck tonight. Maybe I should've waited a couple of more years to get engaged or pushed a little harder last night when asking him where he had been.

"Another one?" the bartender asked.

After glancing over my shoulder toward the back hallway where Ben had disappeared, I frowned and nodded. I didn't expect he'd be coming back out anytime soon.

"Make that two," someone said from beside me. His voice was deep and charming, sending shivers right down my spine.

And when I looked over at him, I knew why. He was one of the handsomest men I had ever seen. Dressed in gray suit pants and an off-white dress shirt that looked to be a size too small—or maybe his muscles were just a bit too big—he had eyes of the devil, a smirk so sinful that I was sure I had only seen it in my nightmares, and luscious black hair that curled over his forehead.

The bartender placed two glasses of Afterglow on the counter. "Here you are, boss."

Boss.

He sat down in the seat beside me, his long leg grazing against mine. "I'm Cristian. I—"

"I'm not interested," I said, cutting him off and glancing over at his godly sculpted face and those intense brown eyes that seemed both cruel and filled with fervor.

While his jaw clenched, he let out a low chuckle that seemed to warm me in all the right places. "I'm not here to hit on you—*yet*. I'm just here to talk, Roxie."

I tensed when he said my name, the sound of it so smooth on his full lips. "Do I know you?" I asked, gripping my glass tighter and trying damn hard not to feel that heat crawling up the insides of my thighs, gathering in my core, making me lust after a man who I didn't call my fiancé.

"I know your boyfriend," he said.

"Fiancé," I corrected.

He curled his lips into another sinful smirk and sipped his drink. "Not for long."

I raised a brow at him, kinda, sorta feeling a little buzzed and really freaking ticked off tonight. Whoever this Cristian was, he had another thing coming. I wasn't about to sit here and take his shit.

"What'd you say?" I asked, placing my glass down.

Cristian looked me up and down slowly, his smirk widening. I expected him to shake his head and tell me to forget about it, that he hadn't said anything, that he was just kidding about it all. But instead, he leaned in closer to me and placed a hand on my knee, his large fingers curling into my inner thigh.

"Not for long," he repeated.

Pressing my lips together, I glanced down at his hand on my thigh and felt my heart lurch in my chest. His fingers were so big, so thick, so rough against my bare leg. He moved them in small, soothing circles and made me clench.

"What the hell does that mean? And why are you touching me?" I asked.

He leaned in even closer to me, his lips grazing against my ear, fingers moving a couple of inches up my inner thigh. He paused for a moment, his low chuckle making me shiver again. "Because I own you now, *principessa*."

I clenched and swallowed hard. "Nobody owns me." Not even Ben.

Cristian pulled away just enough to stare into my eyes with his stormy, dark ones. "Ben didn't tell you yet?" He chuckled down at me. "I didn't really expect him to though. He's a bitch about it."

"Ben is—"

"He's a bitch, an asshole, a fucking *stronzo*." He brushed his finger down my lower lip and gazed at it with so much more damn passion than Ben had *ever* stared at me. "And you know it too, don't you?"

I slapped his hand away. "Ben is not an asshole or a *stronzo* or whatever you just called him. He loves me, and you should probably leave before he comes back out here and finds you touching me like this."

Cristian's smirk just widened even more. "I'm terrified, *principessa*."

I pushed my hands into his chest, feeling the alcohol take over. "You should be. Now, leave me alone."

He stood beside me, towering over me with his bulky frame, and placed his finger under my chin, raising it until I was staring up into the eyes of the devil. "I don't think you understand. I *own you* now, *principessa*. Ben's wrongdoings are yours, and the devil loves making people pay for their crimes." His breath warmed my ear. "Especially sinners like you."

My breath caught in the back of my throat, and I found myself trying to form words … any words … but I couldn't. Something inside of me told me to run as fast as I freaking could, get out of this club, and leave Ben here to burn for whatever he had done to this man.

But I stayed glued to the spot, staring up into the eyes of Manhattan's cruelest devil.

He placed his drink on the counter and nodded to the bartender. "Don't worry about her tab. I got it." And with that, he gave me one last lingering look and turned around, the handle of a gun—*a fucking gun*—sticking out from the back of his waistband.

And from that moment, I knew Ben really had fucked up. We were screwed.

4

roxie

ALMOST AN HOUR LATER, two men walked out of the back hallway and made a beeline for me. I stood, leaving my half-empty glass on the bar, and shuffled through the groups of people having a good time.

Was my first instinct to leave this place behind even if Ben was somewhere in the back? Yes.

I didn't want to be within *any* feet of Cristian or his men.

Glancing over my shoulder, I pushed around people on a mission to get the hell out of here before they could catch me and kill me for whatever Ben had done to them. I bumped into someone's chest and froze. A man about double the size of Ben's tiny frame stood over me.

"Where do you think you're going?"

I swallowed hard. "To the women's room. I … I have to pee." I crossed one leg over the other and pretended to have to pee my goddamn pants, as if some hadn't already leaked out because I was straight-up terrified that tonight would be my last night on earth.

He snatched my arm, his large hand nearly wrapping around

my entire elbow. "You can use the restroom later," he said to me. "Boss wants to see you."

I dug my heels into the ground. "No," I said, shaking my head. "No, please, don't take me back there."

He dragged me through the crowd and down the dark back hallway as I tried so desperately to squirm out of his hold.

"Please, don't. I don't want to die. Please."

He pushed open a door and pulled me into a back alleyway. I squeezed my eyes closed. God, this was really it. We were really done for. I was going to die before I got to do anything that I had been planning to with my life.

When he stopped pulling me, I opened one eye and took a deep breath. There was a car—our car—running in the alleyway, with Ben on the driver's side.

Cristian stood next to him, staring at me with those devilish brown eyes. "*Principessa*, come."

The guard leaned in close. "This won't be the last time we see you."

I yanked myself away from him and smoothed out my shirt, trying to act natural while I felt like the pee was already running down the insides of my thighs. I walked over to the car, Cristian following.

He put his hand on the passenger door handle and smiled. "I will see you *soon*, Roxie."

Crossing my arms over my chest, I waited for him to open my door, and then I slid into the seat and stared through the windshield. "Drive, Ben," I said through clenched teeth when Cristian smacked the back of the car, as if to send us off. "We have a lot of shit to talk about."

As soon as we were off onto the road and merged onto the highway—out of sight of Cristian and his devilish smirk—I smacked Ben on the chest. "What the fuck was that? What kind of trouble are you in?"

"Roxie, calm down," Ben said, gripping the steering wheel until his knuckles turned white. "You don't have to worry about anything, baby. I have this handled. Nothing is going to happen."

I stared at him with wide eyes and pursed my lips, seeing right through his lies. I hated the way he lied to me—the way he *kept* lying to me. It was the one thing I'd told him he could never do in our relationship, yet here I was, letting him lie through his teeth to me.

"Don't shut me out. What did you do?"

Ben slammed his hand against the steering wheel. "Roxie, drop it."

I shifted in my seat. "No, I'm not going to let this go like it's nothing. That man had a gun. *A fucking gun.* And everyone else in that bar, all those guards around him, had guns too." I shook my head. "I don't know why you can't just come out and say it. At least tell me who they were."

Ben blew an angry breath through his nose and took the exit for our apartment. I stared through the windshield and crossed my arms over my chest, twirling my ring around my finger with my thumb. What good was it to marry someone who couldn't tell me when he was in trouble?

We drove into the garage and parked next to a homeless guy sleeping against our neighbor's truck. I cursed myself for ever deciding to move into this apartment building out of every place we could've gone. But at the time, it had been the only place that could fit our budget, especially with all our debt.

"Fine," Ben said after an eternity, voice a breathy whisper. He grabbed my hands. "Those guys are from the Mafia. The Ricci fam—"

The Mafia …

I tore my hands away from his and took a second to breathe.

Cristian was from the Mafia, maybe even the boss himself. He had sure walked and talked like he owned everyone in the club, had the money to buy off anyone to keep them quiet, had guards around him, just waiting to tear off someone's head.

And Ben fucking Goodman owed them something.

"Ben's wrongdoings are yours."

"What did you do?" I asked, unable to believe that Ben—my Ben—had done something so horrendous to get stuck with them breathing down his neck.

What could he have possibly done to get mixed up with men like that?

"Nothing you need to worry about, baby. Just ..." He brushed his fingers against my cheek, and I moved away.

Ben had lied to me. Ben *had* been lying to me for weeks. Weeks! He had to be deep, or he must owe them something fucking huge.

I shook my head. They were going to kill us, fucking kill us.

Ben tried to envelop me in a hug, drawing me closer to him. "I have this all figured out. Everything is going to be okay. You don't have to worry at all."

"And how do you have it figured out? What are you going to do?" I asked, not believing a word he said.

As of today, he had been lying to me, staying out late, and was messed up with the Ricci family, New York's cruelest Mafia.

Though Mafia dealings weren't as prevalent nowadays—especially publicly—they still owned everyone and everything. And the Ricci family was the worst. Growing up, I had heard stories from my grandmother about the horrendous things they had done to my grandfather, all the lies he had spilled to her, all the stories, all the pain.

Ben looked at the console between us. "Just ..." He took a deep breath. "I have it under control. Please, believe me."

I didn't believe him, and I didn't know if I ever could again.

Ben Goodman was a liar. Ben Goodman was indebted to the Mafia. Ben Goodman had gotten us into a world of betrayal, lies, and heartbreak.

5

roxie

"I HAVE TO GO," Ben said at exactly midnight.

No kiss on the cheek. No bear hug. No goodbye.

Just Ben with a stone-faced expression, a gun he had gotten from somewhere tucked into the back of his pants, and a swagger that didn't quite fit him right. It was as if Ben lived this entirely different life after midnight, a life that I would never truly believe was his.

I sank into the bedsheets, watched him walk out of the bedroom, and listened to the front door slam closed. We were fucking screwed for the rest of our lives. There was no way we'd get out of this one. I didn't need an expert to tell me that.

Instead of falling asleep, as I should've done, I rolled over and grabbed my rabbit vibrator from the nightstand drawer, slid it inside of me, and turned it on. I needed something to help me relax. Those glasses of Afterglow were strong, but they hadn't done it for me tonight.

My eyes fluttered closed, and I tried to focus on something other than Ben and his problems because thinking about them would just make it hard for me to come and relax for even a moment. I took a deep breath, letting my toy vibrate against my clit. Waves of pleasure rushed through me, pushed me higher, closer to that edge.

Stomach tightening, fingers tugging on my nipples, breath quickening, I moaned softly.

My thoughts wandered from sweet nothingness to *him*, Cristian Ricci, the cutthroat mob boss who couldn't seem to take his eyes off of me tonight. The way he had walked around his club, down the hall, through the alleyway like he owned the entire world and everything in it.

He was a devil—maybe *the* Devil himself.

I arched my back, turning the vibrator up another setting.

Just as I was about to let today's worries go completely, my phone rang.

It was probably Ben, calling me to see if I was still angry with him for ruining our lives. I tried to ignore it, but it kept ringing and took me out of my state of mind, so I slammed my finger on the Answer button and held the phone up to my ear.

"What?" I snapped.

"Roxie," Cristian said through the phone, his voice so deep that I couldn't forget it. "Still awake?"

My breathing hitched. "How'd you get my number?" I asked breathlessly.

I should've pulled the vibrator out, should've turned it off, should've stopped tugging on my nipples when I answered the phone. But I couldn't … I fucking couldn't. His voice, his words, that gruff expression on his face earlier.

Turning the vibrator up a setting, I closed my eyes. The vibrations came quicker and louder, sending me closer and closer to the edge. I threw my phone beside me and turned it on speaker.

"What do you want, Cristian?" I asked.

He paused. "Are you touching yourself?"

"No," I breathed out, slapping a hand over my mouth.

Fuck. Fuck. Fuck. Fuck. Fuck.

Ben was my fiancé—*my fiancé*—my damn lying fiancé.

I shouldn't be lying in bed and thinking about another man. I shouldn't be pushing my hand between my legs and wondering what Cristian would do if he were here with me. I shouldn't be fantasizing about him so much.

Everything about him screamed danger, yet my body couldn't seem to cool off hours after I had last seen him. The way his eyes locked on mine. The way his lips curled up just a few centimeters. The way he looked at me like I was going to be his one of these days.

"What do you want, Cristian?" I repeated when I knew I wouldn't moan aloud.

"I'm at your door. Answer it."

I turned off the vibrator. "You're at my door?"

The phone went dead.

Fuck. Fuck. Fuck. Fuck. Fuck.

After tossing my vibrator onto the dresser, I pulled on one of my robes and hurried into the living room, not even bothering to turn on the light. When I opened the door, the hallway was empty, bright white light filtering into the room. I stuck my head out the door and looked from side to side. Nothing but the stench of alcohol and piss coming from the apartment diagonal from us.

Someone's hand wrapped around my wrist from behind. Cristian yanked me back into the apartment, shut the door, and pressed me against it, his breath in my ear and his body against mine.

"Wearing this for me, Roxie?" he asked, his fingers trailing against my bare collarbone and pushing the Aerie robe just over my shoulder, letting the moonlight glisten against my skin.

My breath caught in my throat, and I nearly had a heart attack. "What the *hell* are you doing in my apartment?" I asked through clenched teeth, trying hard not to stare into those intense eyes or feel how his knee was slipping between my legs, making my robe spill open just a bit more.

"I came to see you," Cristian said, his eyes wandering back up my body to my face. His lips curled into a soft smile, eyes so dangerous. "But you were busy pleasuring yourself."

I swallowed hard. "I was not."

He chuckled and rested his hands on the door, next to my head, trapping me in. "Your nipples are hard, Roxie. You were either playing with yourself or you're really excited to see me here."

His gaze flickered down to them as I pulled my robe tighter, so he couldn't see my breasts. But my nipples, they were still piercing through the thin material, still aching to be touched.

After brushing his fingers up my arms, he growled lowly. "If I don't leave soon, I'll end up tugging on them, *principessa.*" He drew his nose up the side of my neck and stepped closer to me, his chest pressed against my breasts.

I sucked in a short breath, my chest rising and falling, nipples grazing against his chest. Pleasure rushed through my body, and I let out a small moan. It felt too good. It shouldn't.

"Oh, *principessa,* don't fucking do that to me," he said, grasping my chin and pinning me to the door.

I needed him to touch me so bad—so fucking bad. He slid his knee higher between my thighs until it reached my core and blew an unsteady breath out through his nose.

"You should go," I said. "Now."

After giving me one last long look, he pulled me away from the door, opened it, and walked out into the hall. His jaw twitched, as if he would snap at any moment and take me, throw me up against the wall, and ruin me.

I didn't think I'd let him … but I hadn't thought I'd think about him when I touched myself earlier.

I shut the front door on him, hurried back to my bedroom, shoved my vibrator back up into me, and thrust it into my pussy over and over and over. Pretending like it was his knee grinding against my throbbing core again. Teasing me with all that body heat. Making me … making me come.

A rush of pleasure shot through my body, leaving my legs tingling in delight. I sank into the sheets, feeling my pussy pulse over and over again and trying so desperately to think about anything other than the devil's intense brown eyes.

6

roxie

"I'M LOOKING FOR CRISTIAN," I said, my heart thumping against my chest.

I stood in his club, near the bar, tapping my foot on the ground and chewing on the inside of my lip. I shouldn't be here. I should've been at work, sucking up to my boss to let me off easy after showing up late to work again yesterday because I had stayed up all hours of the night, worrying about my lovely, *honest* fiancé.

The bartender walked over to one of Cristian's many guards. After taking one long look at me, the guard nodded, gesturing to follow him down the hallway. I swallowed hard and fumbled with my fingers.

Why was I here again? I should've been long gone, out of the damn state by now.

I stood a good foot shorter than the man as we walked beside each other down the long corridor and to one of the many back rooms. Sweat dripped down my lower back.

Am I getting dizzy? I have to be getting dizzy. I should go, leave, disappear. *Now.*

Slamming the side of his fist against the door, the guard looked down at me. "Cristian is doing business now. He doesn't like to be interrupted."

My eyes widened, and I shook my head. "Why didn't you tell me? I would've—"

Someone yanked the door open.

"Wh—" Cristian paused mid-sentence, his harsh voice coming to a complete stop as he looked at me, lips turning into a smirk. "*Principessa,* not the woman I was expecting to see this early." He opened the door wider and gestured for me to come into the room even though there was a couple seated in front of his desk.

I swallowed hard and stared between them, realizing that they had the same look as Cristian—the same ritzy, rough Mafia look. As soon as the woman smirked at me, I turned my ass right around to get the hell out of there.

Cristian caught my arm. "Stay," he demanded. It wasn't a question, but a cold and hard order. "I'm finishing up business, but I can attend to you in a few moments."

After walking hesitantly into the room, I took a seat on a couch in the back of the room and gnawed on the inside of my lips.

Cristian walked behind his desk and nodded to another one of his guards. "Get her something to drink. White wine, Afterglow Elixir—her favorite," he said, remembering my drink from the other night.

The man at the desk cleared his throat. "I don't think—" he started in a thick Italian accent.

"It's fine, Alessandro." Cristian turned to the woman and sat down, his gaze on me as I anxiously sat on the couch and wondered why I was here again. "As you were saying, Chiara?"

"I've been cleaning my family up after my father fucked us all and found ties to the Ricci family." She paused and tensed. "Child trafficking up north, probably some of your family from Upstate New York or even in Boston or Providence."

Cristian blew an angry, quiet breath from his nose and cursed under his breath. "I'll look into it." He balled his hands into fists. "Keep me updated with any new information that you learn."

Chiara and Alessandro stood, Alessandro wrapping his arm around Chiara's waist, fingers curling into her side so possessively. Cristian walked them to the door and saw them off, turning to me when they were gone.

He walked over to me, and I stood and stepped back, wanting to keep as much space between us as possible, especially after last night.

"We need to talk," I said.

"About last night?" he asked. Sunlight flooded in through the windows. He shut the blinds and turned back to me with a smirk. "Those pretty little moans of yours had me thinking about you all morning."

I pressed my legs together. *Don't think about it, Roxie.*

"No, not about last night," I got out.

He walked around me, staring me down like he was a fucking hawk and I was the prey he'd scoop up and feast on for dinner tonight. "You look tired. Did you stay up all night, waiting for Ben to come home?" He stopped behind me and leaned in. "Or were you up all night, thinking about me?"

I closed my eyes, taking a shaky breath. "Cristian."

"Roxie," he whispered, lips brushing against my ear, sending a wave of heat through my entire body to my core.

His hands … I could feel them. They were so close to my waist, so close to wrapping around it, dragging me back to his desk, showing me what kind of maniac this man truly was.

This kind and cute act he was giving me was just that—an act. Cristian Ricci wasn't nice. He was cruel. He took what he wanted. He didn't give a fuck about anyone else. And this man would destroy me the same way in bed.

My eyes widened, cheeks flushing. *Oh Lord, I didn't just think that.*

Someone knocked on the door, and the same guard from earlier —the one with the strong grip and cruel smirk—walked into the room. "Mr. Cradle is here to see you about business."

I fixed my purse tighter on my shoulder. "I should go. You're busy."

He snatched me by the upper arm and pulled me back to him. "You're not going anywhere." He looked toward the guard. "Tell him that he has to wait."

I shook my head. "Really, it's fine. I—"

"I make time for people who are important to me," Cristian said as the guard left.

"I'm not important to you," I said.

He moved closer to me and curled a finger around a strand of my hair. "Not yet, *principessa*, but you will be one day." He took my earlobe between his teeth and tugged on it lightly. "One day soon, you'll be mine."

My breathing hitched. "I'm marrying Ben," I gritted out.

But I couldn't help but feel the ache between my legs, driving me higher and higher, wild even. *This isn't okay. This isn't okay. This definitely isn't okay.*

Cristian chuckled and trailed his fingers across my waist like he owned me. "A man who has no money to his name. A man who continues to pile up gambling debt. A man who has taken money from your joint account and will force *you* to pay up."

I pressed my lips together, chest tightening. "You're lying."

"You're in debt," Cristian said, making sure the words hit hard.

"Not anymore," I said.

I had been working my ass off to get us out of the thousands of dollars of Ben's debt. When we had started dating, he had been nothing but a nobody with debt he told me his family had put him through. Sure, he went out a couple of nights a week to play poker with some of his friends, but …

He was lying. Cristian had to be lying.

Ben had been helping me, told me he stopped going out with the guys a year ago. He couldn't fucking be back to doing it. I didn't believe it.

"Why don't you check?" he asked me.

After giving him my best stink eye, I opened my bank app on my phone. It was the joint bank account we had opened up the first night we started talking about marriage. Ben dealt with the bills coming in and out of it, as he had more time and made more money than I did—or at least, that was what he had told me.

When I saw it, my heart dropped.

Nothing. There was nothing inside, except hundreds of messages popping up in a blaring red font about overdraft fees and a negative number—$103,761—due to the bank. To the fucking bank. I didn't know how the hell he had overdrafted that much without the bank closing the account or when it had happened ... but it was there, and it had *my* name on it too.

"No," I whispered, my fingers trembling.

I placed my phone on his desk and shook my head. No, this couldn't be true. We couldn't be in this much debt. I had worked so hard—so fucking hard—to pull ourselves back out.

We were trapped.

Cristian stepped toward me, his breath on the back of my neck. "Say it, Roxie," Cristian whispered into my ear, voice low and husky. "Tell me why you're in my office this early if it isn't because of last night."

"I want you to let him out," I pleaded with New York City's cruelest man, most devious devil, and most seductive Mafia boss. I turned around and stared up into his hard and dead eyes. "Please, forgive his debt to you."

It was our only way.

Cristian gazed at me, then grasped my chin in his hand, pushing me so hard against his desk that I was nearly sitting on it. This ... this was the Mafia boss everyone was terrified of. This was the man who snapped at a moment's notice.

"Why are you asking for forgiveness for him?" he asked through gritted teeth, drawing his thumb down my lips.

"Please, Cristian."

That ache ... that damn ache had reappeared.

"There's one thing and one thing only I'd take to forgive his debt," Cristian said, pressing me against the desk, one leg between my thighs, inching it higher and higher until it reached my core. He loomed over me, all that hard muscle brushing against my abdomen. "Ask me what it is."

My heart raced in my chest, beads of sweat rolling down my back. "What is it?" I whispered, my voice on the verge of cracking and making me sound weak and tired and so fucking scared.

He chuckled in my ear, sending shivers down my back. "You, Roxie. It's you."

7

cristian

"ME?" Roxie whispered, her big brown eyes widening, as if she didn't quite believe it. She crossed her arms over her chest and scratched the black tattoo on her collarbone. "You want me?"

My lips curved into a smirk, and I ground my knee against her core, watching how her eyes flickered down to it and feeling her thighs press together around mine. I brushed my thumb across her jaw.

"Do you want his debt to me to be gone?" I asked into her ear. "Do you want safety at all hours of the day? Money you can spend freely? Vacations you've only ever dreamed of?"

She paused for a moment, glanced down at the mere centimeters of space between us, and took a deep breath. "I don't want to be in debt," she said, voice unusually broken and defeated. Those scared-voiced words sounded so foreign on her fiery tongue.

"You come with me willingly," I said, knowing that it wouldn't be something she could pass up.

What woman wouldn't want to be millions of dollars richer, protected by the cruelest mob boss in all of Manhattan, and have to *beg* to leave his bed?

She swallowed hard, her gaze flickering from me to the door. She shifted uncomfortably beneath me, thighs grinding together, as if her sweet little cunt was just aching for me to press myself into her harder. To make every inch of her *mine.*

I waited. For moments. For minutes. For what seemed like an eternity.

She drew her tongue across her plum–painted lips. "No."

"Excuse me?" I asked, brow arched. *Did I hear her right? Did she tell me no?* "No?"

Roxie shook her head of half-blonde, half-brunette dyed hair. "No, I'm not going with you. Especially not willingly." She pushed her shoulders back and sneered at me, challenging the man who ruled the city and everyone in it. "You'd have to throw me in the back of your car, kidnap me, and kill Ben to ever have me."

My hands balled into fists at the sound of *no.* I always got what I wanted, when I wanted it, where I wanted it. Nobody ever dared to say no to me with such confidence like she had. Nobody ever dared to look me straight in the eyes when they said it too. Nobody ever dared to challenge me the way she had.

People and business deals fell into my lap willingly.

After a couple of moments of staring me in the eye with her wavering gaze, she tore herself away and took a step to the right, turning around to face the other way. "No, Cristian."

I stepped behind her, placed my hands on her shoulders, and squeezed *gently.* "Are you telling me or asking me, *principessa*? Are those your terms and conditions for me to have you in my bed, on my desk, wherever the *fuck* I want you?"

She shuddered and leaned a centimeter toward me, into my touch. Then, she ripped herself away from me again, twirled around, and glared up at me under those mascara-dressed lashes. "Get your hands off me, Cristian," she said through clenched teeth. Her cheeks were flushed, nipples hard against her shirt.

She loved this. She fucking loved this.

If she didn't, she would've stormed out of here by now.

I wrapped my hand around her small throat and shoved her

hard against the desk. "Don't fucking talk back to me, Roxie. I always get what I want, and I want you. If I have to kill your little *stronzo* fiancé to take you, then I will. But … if it comes to that, you're dealing with his debt to me on your own terms. I will own you, *principessa*, for real this time."

She swallowed hard and stared up at me, vein pulsing wildly against my palm. "You're fucking crazy," she said through her pouty, full lips. "Why do you even fucking want me? Is it because you've never found a woman who doesn't want you? Am I a challenge to you? A piece of trash you're going to throw out when you're done?"

Gaining confidence, she pursed her lips. "Huh? Why bother with this at all? You don't even know me, Cristian Ricci."

I stared down at her, jaw twitching. She really didn't know, did she?

Pulling her closer to me, I pressed my lips to her ear. "Tell me why you're still here if you don't want to be. Tell me why your cunt is wet, why you're pressing your thighs together, why you're giving those big brown fuck-me eyes, making me want to put you in your fucking place."

She crossed her arms over her chest and turned away from me, shaking her head. "I'm not," she said after some time, her voice softer this time. "This is a mistake." She clutched her purse. "The bank made a mistake. Ben made a mistake. I made a mistake coming here." She swallowed hard. "Ben loves me."

A mistake.

This wasn't a mistake.

The only mistake she could make was walking out of my office and into Ben's arms.

"Does he love you, or does he need someone to make him feel like a man, like he's wanted by someone he would've never had a chance with if she knew how bad his problem was?" I asked, tapping my index finger against the desk. When she didn't answer me, I leaned in close to her again, taunting *myself* this time. "Answer me."

She paused for a few moments and looked toward the window blinds. "And you think *you* can be that man?" she asked, brow arched. She blew a harsh breath out of her nose. "Highly unlikely."

I rested my hands on the desk beside her, trapping her in, and growled in her ear, "Something that you don't understand, *principessa*, is that I don't need anyone to feel like a man." I pressed myself against her thigh, letting her feel just how hard I was under my suit pants from her bratty mouth. "I'd give you everything you could ever ask for, take you to places you'd have to work hours upon hours to go to, only to find out that your *loving* fiancé gambled away all your savings. I could give you a life you've only ever dreamed of."

8

roxie

I STARED at the engagement ring on the kitchen table with tears in my eyes. I had taken it off two hours ago after I got home from Cristian's club and hadn't been able to tear my eyes away from it.

There were so many things I had dreamed of my life being, but being lied to by a man who didn't love me wasn't one of them. I wanted to throw the ring at the wall, wanted to crush it with my fist, pack up all my bags, and leave this place for good this time.

But without any money and with all this debt, I couldn't go anywhere.

Being stuck somewhere you didn't want to be sucked more than I'd thought it would.

After I sat at the table for another fifteen minutes, wondering where Ben was, our front door finally opened. Ben walked into the apartment, sliding his hand across his face and shaking his head in defeat. Dropping his things by the front door, he let out a long drawn-out sigh and walked into the living room, not even seeing me.

"Where have you been?" I asked from the kitchen, tapping my

fingers against the glass of Afterglow I had devoured once I got home.

There were dark lipstick stains all over it, but I didn't care anymore. I hoped the stains stayed on the damn cup because Ben would loathe it.

Ben jumped and turned around. "Shouldn't you be at work, Roxie?"

"Shouldn't you have told me the truth from the beginning?" I asked, sitting up taller and finally having the fucking confidence and strength to confront him about what he had done to us, to *me*, to our future.

Thrusting his hands into his pockets, he walked over to the kitchen and noticed the ring on the table and my bare hand next to it. He clenched his jaw and shook his head. "Why did you take your ring off?" he asked.

"Why are you gambling again?" I asked back, refusing to let him put this on me.

None of this shit was my fault.

As much as I hated to fucking admit it, Cristian was right. Life with him would be simpler, but my pride wouldn't let me fall into him so easily. Everything told me to run from him. He was the most dangerous man in the city, if not the country. And he wanted me.

Someone he'd never get.

He tensed up, his eyes becoming as wide as a deer in headlights. For me to have taken off my ring … he knew he'd fucked up big time. I'd found out about his little fucking secrets that he'd been keeping from me.

Fuck him. I'd trusted him.

"What are you talking about?" he asked, snatching the ring and my hand. "Put this back on, Roxie. I don't know what Cristian told you, but I have been working my ass off to get him off our back."

Before he could put the ring back on my finger, I yanked my hand away.

"Keep the fucking ring," I sneered through clenched teeth. I balled my hands into fists so hard that my nails dug into my palms, probably drawing blood. "Sell it. Put the money toward the one hundred three thousand dollars in debt we are in. And who the fuck knows how much debt *you* are in with the banks and Cristian?"

"What are you talking about?" he asked again.

Did he really think I was that fucking stupid? Did he think I didn't know, that I wouldn't find out about all his late-night gambling?

"We're not in that much debt. Only a few—"

"I saw the account. You forgot to change the password. You fucking lied to me *and* stole from me, Ben." I shook my head, tears forming in my eyes. But I wouldn't cry, not this time. "We've been together for years. I've been giving you my money to help us out, and you fucking screw me over like this."

Ben got quiet for a long time and shook his head. "Please …"

He grabbed for my hand again. I got up, stepped away from him, and held myself back from hurling the empty wineglass right at his head.

"Please, just take the ring. It means everything to me that you have it," he continued.

I stared down at the cheap piece of rock lying in his open palm. Ben either really fucking loved me and wanted me to have it for myself or the thing didn't have any value to it. I didn't give a fuck how much it was worth, but if it was a fake after he talked for weeks about how he'd saved up for it, I'd lose my shit.

I'd lose my fucking shit.

"I'm not taking the ring back," I said. "Not until you get your shit together and get *me* out of debt the way you put me into it. I'm not going to pay for your mistakes with my money or my life."

Ben stared at me, then turned to the side with the ring in his palm and a sour expression written all over his face. He stormed back to the small table near the door, grabbed his keys, and walked out of the apartment, leaving me to wonder if he'd ever really loved me or if this had all been an act to take my money.

9

roxie

IT WAS ONE A.M., and yet again, Ben wasn't home.

I didn't care though, definitely not tonight because, tonight, I was drunk off half a bottle of Afterglow. I'd wanted to make myself feel good, and I couldn't get all of Cristian's little promises off my mind. It'd be easier with him, but I loathed the man for putting me in this position.

Hell, I didn't even know him. All I knew was the family my grandparents had been terrified of, led by Cristian Ricci's grandfather, who'd come around every other Thursday night to have a *chat* with my grandfather out in the garage.

There had been times he came back into the house with piss running down his leg.

As I stared up at the bland white ceiling and wondered what I had done to get here today, my bedroom door rattled. I found myself sitting up in bed, knowing that it couldn't be Ben home so soon. But maybe it was Cristian back in my house, trying to scare me or get in my bed.

Maybe I'd welcome him because fuck Ben.

I tossed the bottle of wine onto the bed and let it spill out, ruining our blankets.

Instead, I sat back in bed and thrust a hand between my legs, wondering what it would be like if he actually stepped into my room and touched me the way my body was aching for him to. It was so freaking wrong, yet I couldn't stop thinking about him. Earlier, when he had touched me, it had made me tense up, made me want, need, desire him.

When my door rattled again, I hopped up in a tiny nightshirt to rip the door open. I expected to see Cristian in the hallway, but it was two men, dressed in black suits, that I didn't recognize.

Almost instantly, one grabbed me by my throat and shoved me into the bedroom. "Stay in there. We're looking for Ben."

My eyes widened, heart pounding against my chest. "I don't know where he—"

It happened so quickly, the sound of a gunshot ringing out through the apartment.

Holy fuck. Holy fuck. Holy fuck.

I ducked and covered my head, trying to make myself as small as possible. More gunshots, and the guy who had pushed me into the room suddenly rushed into the hallway. I gazed at the window, knowing that I could jump onto the fire escape ... but that damn thing was so old and rusty that I didn't know if it would break when I stepped onto it.

It was either *that* or be killed. So, I made a run for it when, suddenly, the man who had pushed me into the room dropped dead on the hallway floor. I let out a scream and threw the window open.

"Roxie!" Ben said from behind me, a gun in one hand and blood splattered across his work suit.

I turned around, relieved that it was only him but freaked the fuck out that he had just murdered two men in cold blood.

I stared at him. "Who were those men?"

"Ricci family."

My eyes widened. "You killed two men from the Ricci family?! Are you fucking crazy?"

He snatched my wrist in his hand and pulled me out of the bedroom to the front door. "Roxie, we have to go now." He jerked me so quickly that I was stumbling and tripping over my own two feet to keep up.

I stared at the two mobsters, shot dead in our hallway. My heart thumped against my chest, and I shook my head, unable to believe that Ben had gotten us into this mess. We would forever be in the Mafia's debt, would even be killed by them when Cristian found out about this.

"Ben, are you fucking stupid?" I said, tugging him back. "We can't leave!"

After searching their pockets, he grabbed a pair of keys and hurried into the hallway, refusing to let me go this time.

"We have to go," he said, voice final. "He's going to fucking find us the longer we stay here."

I pulled my nightshirt down my body, so the neighbors wouldn't see anything special as he tugged me down the hallway. Everything I'd ever loved and cared about was in that apartment. I couldn't just leave it there.

What were we even doing anyway? Why'd he kill those men? Would I ever get to see my family again—Mom, Dad, my brother? Anyone? If we had to be on the run for the rest of our lives ... I wouldn't.

Instead of taking the elevator, Ben dragged me down the emergency stairs to the garage. I stopped dead in my tracks when we passed our shitty car and he hurried to a shiny black SUV instead.

"You already killed two of his men. We can't steal his car too!" I exclaimed, knowing this was the shittiest fucking idea that I had ever even considered.

"Our car won't make it out of the city," he said. "We can dump this when we get far enough to be free, Roxie. Don't worry about it, just get in."

My eyes widened as Ben pushed me into the car. "What the fuck do you mean, don't worry about it?" I asked.

Everything was happening so quickly, and I really couldn't stay here. They'd kill me or torture me for Ben. Cristian had made that perfectly clear.

"He's going to kill us! You're asking me to leave the state I grew up in, leave my entire life behind, for what?"

Ben started the car, and I didn't know why the hell I was still sitting in it. I should've gotten out and left. I despised every bit of him.

"Roxie, he wanted me to kill someone with a family," Ben said, speeding out of the lot in our shiny, brand-new, stolen SUV.

"Then, fucking kill them!" I said, then immediately clamped my lips together.

What was that, and where the fuck did it come from? I never wanted anyone to die, to be killed. The words had come from fear … fear of not wanting to die and never ever experiencing the life I wanted. It had come from not wanting to be in debt anymore. It had come from wanting to see Cristian again.

Ben looked over at me with wide eyes and shook his head. "I'm going to ignore what you just fucking said. We're leaving, Roxie. And you're staying with me until the fucking end. I'm not letting you go."

10

cristian

"SIR," Giovanni said, hurrying into my office.

I stared at my watch, knowing that Ben should've been back here by now, and cleared my throat. After Roxie had left this morning, I'd been fucking furious about everything that went down. She should've dumped Ben as soon as she found out that he had taken her money. She should've been here, sitting across from me, with those rosy-red cheeks and half-blonde, half-brunette dyed hair cascading down her back.

"What?" I asked, eyes flickering up to him from a file Alessandro had sent over this morning about my family in Boston, who had ties to the child trafficking ring involving the shittiest families in the US. "Is Ben here?"

"Antonio and Piero went to Ben's house to find him, like you'd asked," Giovanni said. He looked nervous, sweating almost. He swallowed hard and looked at his feet. "They're dead now."

I raised my brows. "They're what?"

"And their car is gone. It had some of our shipment for Tuesday in it."

I slammed my open palm against the table. "They're fucking

dead, and Ben took the fucking car?" I stood up and grabbed my gun from the desk, tucking it away into the back of my waistband. "Is that what you're fucking telling me?"

"Yes, sir."

Flaring my nostrils, I tugged him closer by the collar. "I want everyone out looking for them. They're not getting out of this fucking city. Post at every fucking exit, every tunnel, every bridge."

After I shoved him away, he gave me a curt nod, hurried out the door, and started gathering the other guards, who ended up dispersing through the club, heading toward the exits. I slammed my door shut and walked to the windows, pacing beside them and growling to myself.

They had fucking fled town with my shit. Neither one of them would get away with this. Ben would pay with his life, and Roxie ... I might've been nice to her, but now that she was gone with him, she'd pay too.

She'd be mine. I owned her now—really and truly owned her.

I balled my hands into fists and shook my head. Did she think she'd get away from me? I'd find her anywhere she went, would search everywhere to know where she was. She'd never be away from me again.

After I waited ten minutes for something, Giovanni knocked on my door.

"They're en route out of the city," he said.

"Follow them," I said through clenched teeth, grabbing my keys from the desk. "Meet me at the building outside the city where we do business. Blindfold them. Don't let them know where the fuck they're going. I want them to fear for their fucking lives."

Giovanni nodded and disappeared into the hallway. Roxie had told me to take everything from her if I wanted her, and that was what I was going to do. Roxie was about to be mine, whether she wanted to be or not.

11

roxie

"WE SHOULDN'T BE DOING THIS," I whispered to myself, hugging my arms around my body and rocking back and forth in the car. "We shouldn't be doing this. We shouldn't be doing this."

Ben slammed his foot on the brakes, sending me flying forward, my seat belt digging into my chest. "Do you want to get out or not?"

My lips parted, fear running through every one of my veins. "We're too far deep, Ben. We could run for years, and he'd still find us." I glanced in the rearview mirror. "There's no running away from this."

"I'll take care of us," he said foolishly.

Didn't he know who his boss was? Didn't he know that Cristian Ricci didn't take any shit from anyone? How many times had that asshole tortured him? How many times had he continued to follow in his footsteps, and now, he wanted out?

"And how are you going to do that, Ben? Working odd jobs for the rest of our lives?"

He reached in the backseat and grabbed one of the few duffel bags that I thought had his clothes and unzipped it. Cocaine ... the bag was filled with at least $300,000 worth of drugs.

"You fucking stole from the Mafia boss?!" My eyes widened, and I shook my head, staring back at the road in front of us.

This couldn't be happening. This couldn't fucking be happening. We were going to die. He was going to kill us.

"It'll be enough to hold us over until we can get out of the country." He took my hand and began driving once more. "We can start a new life."

I yanked my hand away from him. I didn't want to start a new life with him. He had gotten me deep into this one … and we couldn't just leave. The debt, Cristian's power, Cristian … were enough to make me want to stay. But Ben was going to screw this all up.

After I gazed into the backseat, my heart pounded in my chest. "How many fucking bags did you steal?"

Earlier, when he had told me to get into the car, it was dark. I could barely see into the backseat, but now that I was actually looking … there was at least over a million dollars' worth of bills.

"Relax."

"Stop the car," I said, my knee bouncing.

"I'm not stopping the car, Roxie. He'll find us." Ben pulled off of the main street, heading onto the back roads and into the darkness of the woods.

A black SUV picked up speed behind us, on our fucking tail.

I leaned my head against the headrest, threw my hands over my face, and said, "He already has, you fucking idiot."

Ben hit the gas, speeding deeper into the forest. I stared straight ahead while he looked back at the SUV behind us.

"Ben!" I screamed.

Another SUV pulled right out from another street and stalled in the middle of the road. Ben hit the brakes, just enough to stop the car before we collided.

Four guards with guns hopped out of the SUV in front of us, and three hopped out of the one behind us. All their weapons trained on us. I felt like I was about to have a heart attack, my heart racing faster than it ever had before. I put my hands up in the air, tears streaming down my face.

Someone threw my door open and yanked me out. I fell onto my knees on the harsh concrete, feeling the skin break. Their guns were focused on me as one picked me up by the arm, wrapped a blindfold around my eyes, and tied my hands behind my back.

"I fucking hate Ben," I whispered to myself. "I fucking hate him."

"Shut the fuck up."

Someone pushed me into the backseat of one of the SUVs, and then the SUV did a U-turn and sped through the dark roads. The whole time, my knees were bouncing, my heart was racing, and I wished that they had just killed me there.

I had never been punished by Cristian, but Ben must've been. I had seen the scars on his back and chest. And I'd rather be dead than be waterboarded, than to have my nails pulled off, than to have a knife slide into my flesh.

Yet I sat in that backseat of the SUV, thinking about one thing and one thing only: Cristian fulfilling my *terms and conditions* that I had apparently offered him yesterday. He'd kill Ben tonight, and then that angry, wrathful devil would take me hard.

I pressed my knees together and shifted in the seat, nipples hardening.

"Stop fucking moving," someone said from beside me.

But my core was suddenly pulsing wildly at the thought of Cristian rolling up his sleeves, shoving himself between my legs, and filling me like I had been thinking about every night since I had met him.

After what seemed like a thirty-minute drive, the SUV stopped. The guards pulled me out, dragging my feet on the gravel and into a room. The room was freezing and made all the little hairs on my arms stand up.

I didn't know how many men were here, but I could tell that there were at least several of them.

They pushed me onto my knees, and I tried to hold my tears in.

Why is this happening? Why did I listen to Ben?

Now, I would pay for it with my life.

Through my blindfold, I could see Ben's faint outline fall next to me. Tears raced down my cheeks. Cristian hadn't ever seen me cry before, and I had hoped that it would stay that way … but I couldn't stop myself from crying in front of him for this.

The door opened, and I listened to Cristian's footsteps. He took a deep breath, and I pressed my lips together.

What will he think of me after this? How will he kill me? Quickly, so I don't feel pain? Or slowly, so I pay for everything that Ben has done?

"Take them off," he said in his thick Italian accent.

Someone ripped off my blindfold, the bright lights blinding me. When my eyes finally adjusted, I gazed over at Cristian, who stood a few feet away with a gun in his hand. He stared at me with a clenched jaw and shook his head in disappointment. I gazed at the ground, unable to keep his intense stare. I felt like he saw right through me with it, like he knew every single one of my thoughts, could feel my pain … yet he didn't care.

"Stand," he said.

We stumbled to our feet, and I swallowed hard, unsure of what he would do next.

"Look at him, *principessa*," Cristian demanded.

I swallowed hard, brow furrowed, and glanced over at Ben, the man who had made *me* betray the cruelest Manhattan Mafia boss, the man who once had my heart, the man who had gotten me into this mess.

"What do you see in him?"

What does he want me to say? That I see nothing? That I see a weak man?

"Charm … love … adoration …" he said each word tensely.

I gazed back at Cristian, begging with my teary eyes not to make me do this. "Please …"

He clutched the gun harder in his hand, his jaw tense. "Look at him and tell me what you fucking see, Roxie."

Hesitantly, I gazed back at Ben. "I see the man I once loved."

"What else do you see?" he asked me.

Ben gazed at me, his lips quivering. Though I despised him for putting us into debt, we had spent so much time together, had so many good memories of the past three years. "I see us riding the carousel horses on the boardwalk, running down the beach with the sand in our toes, lying under the stars, and—"

He pulled the trigger, and a bullet went straight through Ben's head. My eyes widened, and I let out a piercing scream, backing away from him. Blood splattered everywhere, Ben's body smacking hard against the ground, a puddle of thick red blood forming under him.

Cristian curled a hand around the back of my head, dragging me closer to Ben's body, and forced me to look at him. "What do you see now, *principessa*?"

I parted my lips, tears streaming down my face. *Oh my God … oh my God …*

He was going to kill me like that too. He was going to leave me in a puddle of my own blood, and nobody would ever find me again.

He pushed me closer to him, his grip never loosening. "What do you fucking see?"

"I … I see … a dead man."

12

roxie

AFTER CHUCKLING MENACINGLY, he pushed me away from him, tilted his head, and stared. I stumbled and clutched the sides of a table, holding myself up. I didn't know what to think. I glanced around the room, seeing the seven other guards blocking all the exits. There was nowhere to run, not that I'd be able to hide from him anyway.

"That will be you next if you don't answer every single one of my fucking questions." He strode closer to me, and I moved back. "Do you understand?"

I nodded. "Yes …"

"Why'd you leave with Ben?"

"I didn't know that he was … he was running from you," I lied.

I grasped a chair, pulling it in front of me to put as much space between us as possible. He snatched it and threw it to the ground, moved over it and stepped toward me.

"Wrong answer."

"I … I left with him because …" *Why did I fucking leave with him again? Because I was a stupid fucking woman.* "Because I trusted him."

He walked closer to me, seized a fistful of my hair in one hand,

and put the muzzle of his gun under my chin. "One last chance to answer me correctly, *principessa*."

My fingers shook, and I stared right into his brown eyes. They were a wrathful kind of dark. A look full of sin and hurt and betrayal and intense anger. I parted my lips and cursed myself for what I was about to say next because even I didn't know if it was the truth or not. "Because I wanted out."

After pulling the gun away from me and tucking it into his waistband, he snatched my chin in his hand, pressing his fingers harshly into me. "You don't fucking get it, do you?" He pulled me closer, and I could feel the imprint of the gun in his waistband. He glared down at me with so much rage. "You're mine, *principessa*. I *own* you."

I nodded, hoping he'd give me some space ... but I knew it wouldn't be that easy. He was going to give me hell for this, hell for trying to leave.

"I can give you a world of so much fucking pain that you would wish I'd killed you with that *stronzo* or I can make you feel good, *principessa*." He tilted his head down at me. "Do I make myself clear?"

I swallowed hard, my whole body tense, and nodded, not wanting to end up like Ben, who was dead on the floor.

He stepped back from me. "Good ..." His eyes raked down my body. "Now, take off your clothes."

My eyes widened. "My clothes?"

"You didn't think you'd get out of this punishment-free, did you?"

He set the chair upright on the ground a few feet away and sat down on it. "You're not going to make me say it again, are you?" He gazed over at Ben on the ground, then back at me and grimaced, as if to say, *I could still kill you, if you'd like.* "Your choice."

I pressed my lips together, staring at all the guards in this room. *Fuck this fucking guy.* I tugged off my shirt and pulled off my pants, standing in just my bra and underwear in front of the Mafia boss himself and seven of his closest guards.

"Tick tock." He looked into my eyes, waiting for me to continue.

Before I could let out a growl, I hesitantly unclipped my bra and let it slide down my arms, my breasts bouncing out of it. I watched the men peer over and tried to ignore the heat pooling between my legs. I pushed down my panties and stepped out of them, covering my breasts with my arms.

"Arms down," he said.

I took a deep breath, my pussy clenching, and let my arms hang by my sides. He stared at my body for a long time, just taking in every inch, lingering on my tits and my throbbing pussy, and then his lips curled into a smirk.

"*Principessa*, you're not ever going to do anything foolish like that again, are you?"

"No," I said, my voice cracking.

"No?"

"No, sir."

"And why's that?"

"Because …" I took a deep breath. "You own me."

"That's right," he said. "I choose who gets to put their cock all the way down that fragile throat of yours. I choose who gets to fuck your tight little ass." He glanced at his guards. "I can let them all fuck you right here while I watch, and you can't say anything about it. Do you understand?"

I pressed my lips together, my heart racing.

When I didn't say anything, he cleared his throat, stood, and walked over to me, posturing over my naked body. "Do. You. Understand?"

I nodded. "Yes, sir."

"Good."

He paused for a long moment, stepped away from me again, eyes never leaving mine, and then he tilted his head in the direction of one of his guards. "Marco, you know what to do."

The guard walked over to me, and my eyes widened.

Oh my fucking God. This guy is absolutely psychotic. He wasn't fucking kidding.

I backed away, shaking my head, yet the heat in my core grew hotter. The guard, Marco, was the same one from this morning and must've been one of Cristian's closest. He was big, brawny, and absolutely terrifying. I stared at Cristian as Marco tugged off his shirt, undid his belt, and pushed down his pants. Cristian's eyes were clouded with anger and rage.

"Anywhere but her pussy, Marco." He smirked at me. "Her pussy's mine."

Marco picked me up, sat on the table, then placed me right on top of him, my back against his chest. I pulled my legs together, trying to hide my pussy from all the other guards and from Cristian. I didn't want him to know that … whatever he was planning … wasn't a punishment for me.

Marco spread my legs, placing my feet on the opposite sides of his thighs so *everyone* could see my glistening pussy, and pressed himself against my ass. My pussy tightened, readying for the punishment I was about to get. He pushed himself inside of me, and I squirmed in his arms, my breasts bouncing. He dug his fingers into my sides and held me in place. I gazed up at the bleak ceiling.

Fuck. Fuck. Fuck. Fuck. Fuck. He was so big—his arms, his body, his cock.

"Eyes on me, *principessa.*" I could hear the smirk in Cristian's voice. "I want to see that pretty face of yours before I let my men ruin it."

I gazed over at him, my brow furrowed. He stared at me like he owned me—because he did—and placed his hand on his thigh. I glanced down at his light-gray suit pants, seeing the imprint of his cock against it. God, I never thought this would happen.

"Spread her legs, Marco. I want to see how desperate her pussy is for a cock," he said.

Marco curled his arms under my legs and spread them wider, so the guards could watch his cock ram into my ass. With every thrust, my tits bounced. Marco grasped one in his hand, tugging on my nipple. Cristian gazed at me, his jaw clenching slightly.

I tried to suppress my moans, but the pressure was too much. I opened my mouth to let out a small whimper but couldn't stop myself from screaming instead. Marco groaned under me, thrusting his cock harder into me. And I continued to moan, louder and louder each time. I'd been waiting so long for this.

Cristian nodded to another guard, who walked over to me, kneeled on the table with us, pulled down his pants, and forced his cock down my throat. I gagged on it as he tangled his hand in my hair, face-fucking me.

I looked over at Cristian, like I knew he wanted me to, and moaned on the guard's cock, my pussy clenching over and over and over. God, I needed Cristian inside of me, thrusting his cock deep into my pussy, filling me up, taking me. It was the thought that I'd been touching myself to for the past couple of days.

He nodded to one of his other guards, who walked over to me, knelt on the table, and pulled out his cock too.

"Why don't you take another one?" Cristian said, walking closer to me.

One of the men thrust into my mouth a few times, then the other, then back and forth, over and over while he stalked toward me, drawing his fingers up the insides of my thighs and teasing me.

"Who's letting you feel good?" Cristian asked me.

I gagged on one of their cocks, spit dripping out of my mouth, and tried to answer. But when nothing coherent came out of my mouth, he slapped my pussy hard with his hand.

"Who's making you feel good?"

The guard pushed himself all the way down my throat, and Cristian wrapped his hand around my neck, squeezing tightly. My cheeks flushed, and I stared up at him with tears in my eyes. My pussy clenched. I parted my lips to try to say something, but nothing could come out, except more spit and a sloppy, wet gagging sound.

He slapped my pussy harder, and I gagged again. The guard pulled his cock out of me, and I gasped for breath.

Cristian wrapped both his hands around my neck, forcing me to look at him. "You don't want to know what happens if you make me ask it again."

"You," I breathed out. "You, sir."

He nodded and loosened his grip on my neck. One hand wandered down my body to my pussy, and he plunged a finger into it. I immediately clenched around him, my pussy desperate for anything to be inside of it right now.

"Are you ever going to betray me again?" he asked.

He stuck another finger inside of me, and I shook my head.

"No, sir." My pussy tightened even more.

"What do you say when you want something from now on?" he asked.

"Please," I said.

"And what do you want now?"

He knew exactly what I wanted. For him to fuck me.

"For you to put your cock inside of me," I said.

He roughly brushed his thumb over my lip, tilting my head to the side.

"Please, sir," I said, gazing up at him through my lashes.

He undid his belt, pulled himself out of his pants, pushed the head of his cock against my wet pussy, and then shoved himself inside of me.

My pussy tightened around him, shaping to his size.

He groaned, eyes closing. "*Principessa*, I've been waiting for you to fuck up for so long."

He grasped my thighs, holding them apart, and pumped into me slowly. One of his hands slid down my thigh, and he harshly rubbed my clit, pumping faster into me.

The pressure was already starting to build in my core, and I curled my toes, letting them use me. I loved it so fucking much that I couldn't even think about anything that had just happened. Just him and them and the heat in my core.

His fingers moved quicker around my swollen clit, my juices getting on them. Marco grasped my breasts from behind and squeezed both of my nipples between his fingers. My body jerked up into the air, and I screamed out as the pleasure pumped out of me.

My legs shook in Cristian's hands, yet he didn't stop thrusting into me. Instead, he pumped harder and faster, giving me every-thing he had. And, fuck, he had a lot. One of the guards thrust his cock into my mouth and all the way down my throat, pumping in and out of me.

Cristian wrapped his hand around my throat. "Scream for me, *principessa.*"

I parted my lips, screaming as loud as I could with his guard's cock in my mouth. The man curled his fingers into my hair, using my head to thrust in and out. Cristian moved his fingers faster against my clit again, his hand tightening around my throat even more.

"Are you going to come again?"

I furrowed my brow and nodded, spit dripping down my chin. He slapped one of my tits hard with his hand, and I came undone again. My legs shook, and I screamed for him while gagging on one of his men's cocks.

Marco stilled under me and pulled out of me, his cum dripping out of my ass as the other guards pulled out of my throat. Cristian grabbed me by the arm, forced me onto my knees, and pushed his cock down my throat. "Taste yourself," he said.

I gazed at him through my lashes, my full lips wrapping around his cock. Then, I sucked off all my juices. He groaned, stilling inside of me, then slowly pulled out, his warm cum dripping off my lips and onto my tits.

He smirked down at me, pulled up his pants, and redid his belt. "*Mine.*"

13

cristian

AFTER FUCKING Roxie until she could barely stand, I glanced at Marco and nodded to a half-dazed Roxie. "Take her."

She scrambled to pull on her clothes and hide her body from all the men who had seen it already.

"Don't fucking touch me," she sneered at Marco, ripping her arm away from his when he grabbed it. She crossed her arms and walked to the door she had come in through. "I can walk myself."

"Then, fucking walk," I said to her, gesturing to an SUV. I looked at some of my other trustworthy men. "Take the drugs and secure them. I have business to deal with at the family house. Marco, you're with me."

Roxie growled and slid into the backseat. I glanced into the rearview mirror at her, but she kept herself turned away from me the entire time to stare out the window. "I fucking hate you," she said under her breath but loud enough for me to hear. The way she tried to get my attention was *almost* cute, if it hadn't been for her fiancé trying to steal half my shipment for tomorrow.

Marco drove us to the house as I put on a pair of sunglasses and glanced at Roxie through the rearview mirror. No more Mr. Nice

Guy. She had decided she didn't want that when she left with that fucking asshole late last night.

Now, I vowed to be the cruel Mafia boss she thought I was.

And if she wanted out of her debt, she'd prove it to me by doing the one thing Ben hadn't had the fucking guts to do. It would be her first assignment as the bratty new addition to the Ricci family.

When Marco pulled up to the house, I started toward it, where guards were already waiting for me.

"Bring her to the basement," I said. "She's going to watch everything that happens around here from now on."

Marco grabbed Roxie forcefully this time and pulled her down the stone steps on the side of the house toward the torture chambers, where Charlie was waiting for his punishment for taking all those children to his bedroom and forcing them to touch him in ways a child never should.

I turned the lights on in the creaky, musty chambers.

Slumped against a concrete wall, Charlie opened his eyes and stumbled to his feet. "Cristian," he said, voice old and dried the fuck out. "I'm glad you're here. We need to talk. I didn't do anything."

As soon as the blatant lies spilled out of that man's mouth, I looked at another one of the guards. "Take him out and put him on the cross."

Charlie looked back and forth between me and the torture cross, shaking his head. "Please, don't do this. I'm innocent, Cristian. You have to believe me."

The guards hooked his wrists to either side of the big X-shaped wooden beams, which leaned against the concrete wall.

Just as I walked up to him, Marco and Roxie emerged from the door. Roxie stopped dead in her tracks, swallowing hard and looking at Charlie tied up. I pulled up a chair for her and gestured for her to sit at the side of the room. Breathing rapidly, she hesitantly sat and gripped the arms.

"A woman shouldn't be down here, watching you torture your own uncle, Cristian," Charlie said to me, staring Roxie up and down like she was a piece of fucking meat.

But I wasn't taking any shit from anyone today. I was still pissed the fuck off that Roxie had had the fucking audacity to leave with that fucking asshole.

I grabbed the power drill from the tools lined up, deciding to give him hell. "She watched me kill her fiancé," I said to him, clicking the drill on. "This will be icing on the cake for her, Charlie."

Roxie flared her nostrils at me from the side of the room, crossing her arms over her chest and giving me the death glare she had given me before I fucked it out of her earlier.

"How many fucking children?" I asked, walking toward him.

"None," Charlie spat, struggling to get out of his restraints as he stared at the power drill.

He deserved to burn for this, and I was the Manhattan devil.

I placed the drill bit on his kneecap and turned the drill on the lowest setting, so he could feel every ounce of pain. The drill bit sank into his flesh, twisting and ripping away the first few layers of skin and sinking into his muscle.

Charlie pleaded for me to stop, his body convulsing under the restraints. Blood splattered everywhere. Chunks of muscle flung in every direction, one piece landing at Roxie's feet. She screamed and jumped back.

I stopped the drill and stared her in the eye. "Watch me, Roxie. I want you to know what will happen to you if you disobey me like your fiancé did."

Turning back to Charlie, I snatched his chin. "How many children?"

"I told you, I didn't do anything!" he shouted at me.

After starting the drill again, I placed the drill bit on his other kneecap and drilled until I heard the bone crack. Charlie screamed out, tears streaming down his blotchy, red face. This man disgusted me more than my own father had.

"Twelve!" Charlie shouted as I rested the drill bit on the chelidon of his arm. "There were twelve. Please," he pleaded. "Please, stop and let me go. I fucking promise you, I won't do it ever again."

"Twelve," I repeated to him, pulling away the power drill. "That's all?"

Charlie calmed back down and nodded. "That's all, Cristian. You see? Nothing to get all worked up for. We can call this quits, and you can let me go. We'll have some drinks and shit-talk, like we always do. No hard feelings."

I turned to Marco. "Get me the mirror," I ordered.

He disappeared into the other room for a few moments and reappeared with the floor-length mirror I always used in times like this.

Charlie shook his head and started to really shake the beams.

I poked the drill against his stomach. "Twelve holes isn't a lot. Twelve holes is nothing. When I'm finished, we can call it quits, have some drinks, and shit-talk, like we always do," I said, sending his words right back at him. "Right?"

"Fuck you, Cristian," Charlie said, spitting at me.

After wiping the glob of spit off my cheek, I walked over to Roxie, grabbed her shoulder, and pulled her in front of that desperate old man.

"Twelve holes," I said, squeezing her shoulder. "Where should they go?"

She shuddered underneath me, trying to stay strong and confident, like she always was, but I could see that fear in her eyes.

She swallowed hard and crossed her arms over her chest. "I want to go home."

When she hadn't given me the answer I'd wanted, I pressed my lips together and released her. "You're mine now, Roxie." I pushed her back down into her seat and turned around to Charlie, rage rushing through my veins. "One in each of your balls. One through your tiny little cock. Two in your head. The rest I'll put where I think they look best."

With the mirror placed directly in front of him, I smiled at Charlie's pathetic reflection, placed the drill bit right on his right testicle, and started the drill, drilling right through the skin and pinning it to his pelvic bone. He screamed out in pain, the vein under his left eye pulsing.

"Watch yourself," I ordered, drilling into his other testicle. "You're a pathetic excuse for a Ricci."

And when I finished there, I kept my promise and drilled a hole through his tiny dick.

Screams of terror echoed through the cellar. Roxie stared in horror at Charlie with wide brown eyes, her black mascara stained on her cheeks from earlier this morning. She shook her head, tears welling up in her eyes. Full plum-colored lips parted, she dragged her chipped nails across the tattoos on her forearm.

"His hands," Roxie spoke up. I glanced over at her, but she just stared at Charlie with distaste, shaking her head some more. "So he can't touch anyone again."

I drilled one hole into each of his palms, and then, for good measure, I drilled them into his thumbs at the knuckles until they both split open and fell off.

"That makes seven so far, Charlie." I slapped him across the face. "Was it fucking worth it? Huh?" I slapped him harder, and his head slammed against the wooden beam. "Were all those late nights fucking worth it?"

When he didn't answer me, I ripped open his shirt and decorated his chest with three more holes. I placed the drill down on the table and sorted through the other tools lying on it.

Picking up two nails and a hammer, I walked to Charlie and placed the tip of the nail on his temple. "Remember this," I said to him, slamming the hammer against the top of the nail and impaling it into his head.

Charlie spit up blood, being the dramatic piece of shit he always was. I held out the hammer for Roxie to do the honors on the other side, but she just looked away, disgusted, with more tears spilling down her cheeks. I blew a breath out of my nose and impaled the last nail into the other side of his head.

I'd get someone to patch him up later.

"*Sei bello*," I said, slapping his cheek. "*Bello, bello.*"

14

cristian

CHARLIE WASN'T DEAD YET. He would watch the blood leak out of each hole day in and day out, suffering until I ended his life for good. After what he had done, he didn't deserve a quick death, but a long and agonizing slaughter.

I placed the hammer down, readjusted my tie, and nodded to the door. "Come with me, Roxie," I said to her. Yet she sat there with her arms crossed over her chest, like the brat I thought she was. "I'm taking you home."

She hopped up quicker than I'd thought she would and hurried to the door, brushing past me and nearly running to the car. She slid into the passenger seat, buckled herself in, and stared emptily at the windshield.

After ordering my men to clean up this little mess Charlie had made, I slid into the driver's seat and started the forty-minute drive to Manhattan. Throughout the entire ride, Roxie didn't say two words. I expected her bratty little mouth to say something, yet she didn't look angry or scared about what had happened today.

Just numb.

Instead of heading to her apartment, I pulled into the garage of the building where I slept most nights after coming home from the club and guided her up to her new home. This was close to the club, where I spent most of my time, and I didn't have to drive forty minutes to the main house every morning and evening.

"What's this?" Roxie asked, stepping into a high-rise apartment two floors down from mine. She crossed her arms at the foyer, trying to look as if this were the filthiest place she had ever lived, like she hadn't just come from a shithole.

I shut and locked the door behind us and handed her the keys. "It's your home now."

She shook her head and handed me the keys back. "I'm not living here. I want to go back to my apartment. All my clothes and essentials are there."

She tried to walk past me, but I pushed her back into the living room.

"You live here. I'll take you shopping for new clothes this weekend. You'll have to deal with what I have here for you right now," I said through clenched teeth. "Now, walk into the fucking apartment, take your shoes off, and thank Ben because you wouldn't have gotten here without him."

She flared her nostrils. "Fuck you."

After kicking off her shoes, she stomped to the living room and looked out the floor-to-ceiling windows toward the city. Though she tried to come off as an angry little woman, she glanced down with admiration at the city as it dazzled in the afternoon sun. She'd never experienced such a sight with Ben.

A few moments passed, and she walked back to the living room. She picked up the file I had tossed on the glass table.

"What's this for?" she asked, flipping the file open.

There was a single piece of paper inside of it with the name of the man I had *politely* asked Ben to take care of. He had chickened out of what was meant to be a simple job. Now, the job got passed on to Roxie, so she could prove herself to me.

"The man you will kill," I said.

All the blood drained from her face. She snapped the folder shut and slammed it onto the glass table. "Are you fucking insane?" she asked me, lips curling up in disgust. "I'm not killing anyone. Aren't women in crazy fucking Mafia families not supposed to do shit? Don't they lounge around with money as men like you ruthlessly murder people in their sleep?"

I chuckled lifelessly at her and stepped toward her. "Did you mistake me for a regular old mobster?" I asked, grabbing her by the neck and pinning her to the wall. "You should know better than that, *principessa*. Everyone in this family earns what they have, and all you have now is Ben's debt piled up."

She struggled beside me, trying to break out of my grip. "It's not *my* debt."

"It is now," I said, placing my foot between her legs and pushing my knee between her thighs. I moved closer to her and let my nose trail up her neck, making her shudder. "And let's get one thing straight, *Roxie*. When you left my office yesterday, you were set on not being my woman. If you had decided differently, Ben would still be alive, and you wouldn't have to work for my trust."

With her cheeks flushed red, she clenched her jaw. "I hate you."

I grasped her hand and placed it against the bulge in my pants. "You could've had this pressed against your dripping cunt every night," I said, letting her feel my cock inside my suit pants.

After glancing down between us, she tensed and pulled her hand away.

I grabbed the gun from my waistband and rested the muzzle against the bottom of her chin. "Instead, you have this, *principessa*, always aimed at these cute, bratty lips of yours," I said, drawing my fingers lightly down her plum-painted lips, watching the way they moved for me.

Roxie sucked in a breath and pressed her lips together, probably so she wouldn't say anything stupid and get herself in even more trouble. I stepped away from her, cracked a smirk, and shoved the gun back into my waistband.

"If you need me, I'm two floors up," I said, walking to the door. Just as I was about to walk out, I turned around and looked at Roxie, who hadn't moved an inch, fear in her eyes. "Oh, and, Roxie? I expect the job to be done by tonight."

15

roxie

WHEN CRISTIAN FINALLY LEFT, I let out a breath and slumped my shoulders forward. Alone for the first time today after everything that had happened—from Ben to that disgusting pig Charlie, who Cristian had mutilated and left alive to suffer.

What was worse was that I found myself feeling sorrow for Ben.

He had known exactly what he was getting *us both* into when he decided to take money from the Mafia. Now that he was gone, I had to deal with the consequences of his actions. I still felt a pain in my heart for losing the man I had spent the last few years with, but—as much as I hated to admit it—nothing more.

I'd made my decision when I took off my ring last night.

Walking around the apartment, I sucked in a sharp breath and stared down at the city below me. Never had I thought I could live somewhere like this, somewhere in the heart of Manhattan with more than one bedroom, two floors, a full kitchen, granite counter-tops ... the list went on and on and on.

But I didn't want to stay here for long. I wasn't going to be in more debt to that devilish man. I'd pay my debt any way he wanted me to now and leave him for good because how could I live a life where my significant other brutally tortured people the way he had done to Charlie earlier?

Well, if they deserved it …

I sucked in a breath at my own thought and shook it away, deciding on a quick shower before going to work. I had already missed half the day so far. One more day like this, and I'd be fired for good. I couldn't miss any more time.

After I found some clothes to wear in the closet—which had been made for someone with a petite frame and *not* someone like me with boobs, an ass, and curvy thighs—I hurried out of the apartment to find Marco standing outside my door, leaning against the wall and scrolling through his phone.

My eyes widened slightly as I rushed past him. He shoved the phone into his pocket and followed me to the elevator.

"Where are you going?" he asked.

I clicked the elevator button and waited impatiently, tapping my foot on the ground. "What are you doing, following me?" I asked through clenched teeth, feeling warmth pool between my legs at the thought of how he had touched me so ruthlessly earlier, picking me up like I weighed nothing, spreading my legs for all to see, and sticking his huge cock into my ass.

Heat crawled up my neck, and he stepped into the elevator with me.

"You're part of the Ricci family. You don't leave my sight," he said, crossing his big arms over his chest.

Great. So, now, I have a damn bodyguard.

After waiting for the elevator to take me to the bottom floor, I started my walk toward work. It was a swift ten-minute walk in the city on a sunlit late afternoon—so much shorter than when I'd lived in the other apartment. And Marco followed me the entire time, standing a few feet away, but never losing me among all the people crowding the streets.

The doors were locked when I reached the contracting firm

where I worked. I stupidly knocked twice on the front door and impatiently waited for my boss, Roger, to open the door. He peeked his head out and looked at Marco behind me.

"Didn't you get my call?" he asked me, thick gray brow furrowed.

"No," I said. My phone was still in the SUV that Ben had stolen.

Roger stepped out of the building and closed the door behind him. "You're fired, Roxie."

I shook my head, unable to register what he had said. "What the fuck do you mean?"

He swallowed hard and scratched the back of his neck, glancing back at Marco. "You're fired." He stepped closer to me, sweating. This man was sweating. "Don't show up here ever again, or so help me, they'll kill me."

"You can't just fire me," I said, shaking my head. "I've worked for the past two weeks, and I haven't been paid. I have clients and people to—"

Roger pulled out a wad of cash and thrust it into my hand. "Take all of it and don't contact me again. Your clients will go to another coworker." He reopened the door and shrugged. "Sorry."

My hands clenched into fists as he closed and locked the door behind him. I stomped through the streets, pushing past Marco and right into Cristian Ricci's fucking club. Though it was nearly five p.m., the bar was already starting to fill up with people after work.

I hurried past everyone to the back room, where Cristian's office was, and walked right into the room without an invitation. Cristian sat at the table with the same two people from the other day—the woman and man who were in Cristian's office.

This time, I didn't care who they were to Cristian.

"You fucking got me fired," I sneered through my teeth. "How the hell am I supposed to pay Ben's fucking debt when you got me fired from the job I had worked relentlessly at for the past three fucking years, Cristian?!"

The woman cleared her throat, stood up, and grabbed her man.

"Excuse us. This seems like a private matter." Then, she said to me, "Enjoy your time with Cristian."

I slammed the door closed behind her and locked it *on him* this time.

Cristian tilted his head, still sitting in his chair, and tapped his pen against his cheek. "Did you finish the job I gave you in the manila folder? Bullet straight through the head?"

"Fuck that job. I already told you I wasn't going to kill anyone for your stupid fucking family," I said, slamming my hands on his desk and curling my fingers into the papers there, crumpling them in my hands.

He grasped my wrist and yanked me forward, making me collapse onto the desk with my chest flat against it. "I told you that you work for me now, not a contracting firm. You kill who I tell you to kill. You take what I tell you to take. You do *whatever the fuck* I want you to do, *principessa*."

Kill? I couldn't kill someone. I couldn't steal or hurt or sell cocaine to drug dealers, but I could flirt. And if I had to flirt with Cristian to get out of this entire mess, then I would. It helped that the devil was handsome.

Flirt, Roxie. All you have to do is flirt.

I blew a breath out of my nose, turned around, and grabbed his tie, curling my finger around it. "Let me repay the debt some other way," I whispered to him, letting my finger trail up his throat to his chin. I pushed my breasts together and bit my lip softly. "I know you'd much rather have me in your bed than out on the streets."

While Cristian looked *flustered*, he grabbed my hand and tore it off him. "Nice try, Roxie. Almost tempting."

I pressed my lips together and yanked myself away from him, throwing away my flirting plan. He was supposed to say yes, supposed to fucking fall to his knees for me, like he basically had been since I knew him.

"I'm not going to touch you like that until you finish the job," he said to me.

Balling my hands into fists, I pushed away from him and turned on my heel. Well, I guessed I would have to step up my game because there was no way I'd touch a gun and do his dirty work. But maybe Marco would.

16

cristian

IF IT WASN'T for her blatant disrespect and defiance, the amount of feistiness in Roxie would almost be cute. She stormed to the door, swaying her hips from side to side and sending me that fiery death glare she had given me too many times today.

It had taken everything inside me to vow to keep my hands off her.

I knew I wouldn't be able to last long. I had wanted to run my hands all over her body since the moment I had seen her with Ben when he first took money from me without paying it back. At that time, I was going to kill him, take her with me, and lock her in the family home, but I decided against it, vowing to myself that I would get Roxie another way.

But years passed, and I grew impatient, waiting for her.

Roxie had always seemed to slip out of my hold, even before Ben. She didn't remember who I was or how my grandfather used to bring young me over to her grandparents' place to play with her when our grandfathers did business in the garage.

She had always had boys fawning over her and taking her away from me.

Not this time.

Now, Roxie was mine, and I wouldn't let her go.

"Watch her," I instructed Marco after she marched off through the bar.

When I shut the door behind her, I blew out a deep breath and leaned against the wall. My pants were tight, my dick throbbing hard inside of them. I undid my belt, stuffed my hand into my pants, and stroked myself.

Closing my eyes, I imagined finally losing it and taking Roxie for myself. I had watched her grow up, checked on her whenever I could, held myself back for so long because I knew that Roxie deserved more than this life. She deserved someone who didn't relish in the thought and feeling of torturing a man like Charlie; of watching the life drain from someone's body, like it had with my father; of screwing up people's lives, like mine had been fucked with since birth.

After spitting on my hand, I locked the door and pulled my cock out of my pants. Fingers curling into the paint on the wall, I grunted and jerked my hand faster, lost in the thought of her.

One fucking day, I'd say fuck it, throw the anxiety and fear aside, and fuck her in my bed until she begged for my children.

Someone knocked on the door.

"Cristian?" Alessa said.

I stroked faster and imagined Roxie on her knees, taking my cum on that pretty face of hers, those big brown eyes staring up at me, her cheeks flushed a rosy red.

"Cristian?" Alessa said again. "Are you in there?"

"I'm busy," I said to her through clenched teeth.

She hummed on the other side of the door. "I can help you with that, darling. Open up."

As I stroked faster, she wiggled the doorknob to try to open it. I blew an angry breath out of my nose and pulled my pants back up before I could finish. As soon as I was out of here, I'd be at Roxie's door tonight to end this.

"What the fuck do you want?" I asked after ripping the door

open, glaring down at my sister's best friend, who only fucking liked her because of the money, the guys, and the access to the Mafia's protection.

Alessa closed the door, strolled into the room like she owned it, and hopped up onto my desk, her blonde hair thrown up in a messy bun. "I wanted to come see you. I heard through the grapevine that you have a new friend." She pinched her lips into a tight smile. "Roxie? Is that her name?"

"She's none of your fucking business."

She laughed. "Everything you do is my business."

"How many times do I have to fucking tell you that we were never exclusive?" I asked. "We've been over for two fucking years. Drop the little act you've been putting on with my sister." I tore the door open and gestured for her to leave. "Out."

After a humph, she hopped back off the desk and sauntered to the door, drawing her fingers around my collar. "She's pretty feisty too. Just how you like them," she said. "She'd better be careful."

"You think about touching her, I will kill you."

She let go of my collar and walked down the hall. "I won't touch her, Cristian. Not yet."

I watched her disappear and growled to myself. I had to get Roxie a fucking gun. If she was going to be the coldhearted killer that my father had made me, she needed to know how to protect herself, especially from people like Alessa.

17

roxie

INSTEAD OF HEADING straight home like I should have, I walked up to the bar and demanded that they give me the strongest drink they had. When the bartender asked me for my card, I snatched the drink away from him and told him that the owner would be kind enough to pay for me. I wanted to get hammered after today, but didn't have any money to my name.

I slid onto one of the barstools, glancing up at Marco staring at me from across the bar. I wasn't killing any man tonight or tomorrow or even the next day. Cristian couldn't get me to do it even if he threatened me with death. There was absolutely no way that I'd let him control me like he had with Ben.

That was why Marco would do it for me. I'd do anything that I had to do to get him to comply. Flirt with him behind Cristian's back, sleep with him behind Cristian's back, blow him behind Cristian's back. But first, I'd ask nicely.

Because I didn't want to be on my knees for a man just to get him to do my dirty work.

If he said no, then I'd—

"Cristian isn't a bad guy," someone said, taking a seat next to me.

Glancing over, I noticed that same brunette woman from Cristian's office. Chiara, I thought her name was. She asked the bartender for a glass of sambuca, sipped it, and looked over at me. Between the Chanel handbag, dress, and jewels dripping off her body, everything about her screamed Mafia.

Of course she wouldn't think that he was a bad guy. She and her boy toy must do the exact same thing—deal drugs, swim in million-dollar pools, not a care in the world, and murder people while they slept.

"You can't talk," I snapped at her. "You're just like him, aren't you?"

Her eyes widened, as if she was surprised, and then she smiled at me. "Cristian will have his hands full with you. You're a feisty one. Not many people have big enough balls to talk back to him the way you did back there."

After taking another gulp of my drink, I shoved the glass to the bartender. "Another one." When he placed another glass on the counter, I turned to her with my brows drawn together. "He killed my fiancé, kidnapped me, and forced me to lose my job. Why wouldn't I be pissed at him?"

She smiled and took another sip of her sambuca. "He deserves for you to be pissed at him. He's a good guy, but he can be a dick. All men in the Mafia are—until they find that one woman who is brave enough to put them in their place." She pushed the half-empty glass to the edge of the counter and stood. "And I think Cristian has finally found his match."

I gave an ugly snort of a laugh and turned back to the bar. *What a joke.* This woman actually thought that *I* had the hots for the cruelest man in Manhattan, thought that I could change him to be a better person.

"You don't have to believe me," Chiara said, grabbing her purse. "You will eventually. And as you're going to be here quite often, you're going to need a friend. The family whores will try everything to get with Cristian. I've seen it up close."

My hands balled into tight fists at the mere thought of it. Chiara looked down at my hands and smirked, knowing she had gotten me to expose my true thoughts about all of this. I unclenched them and grimaced at her.

"I'm Roxie," I said.

"Chiara," she said, stealing my phone away and putting in her number. "Call me anytime."

When she walked away, I stared back at her and thrust my phone back into my pocket. "Another drink, please," I said to the bartender.

He eyed my empty glass and reluctantly gave me another one. I drank it down, not wanting to even feel for the rest of the day.

Cristian walked out of his office and around the bar, whispering something to Marco. He made eye contact with me, and I tore my gaze away and clenched my jaw. I hated the man for making me do what *Ben* should've done before he got murdered.

I couldn't kill someone. I couldn't put a bullet through someone's head. I couldn't tear families apart the same way that the Ricci family had done to my grandfather. Cristian had to have a good fucking reason for wanting this man dead if he wanted an outsider to kill him.

When Cristian disappeared back into his office, I blinked a few times to reorient myself. All I could feel was the alcohol coursing through my veins, making me woozy. Just how I'd wanted it to. If I could just forget today had ever happened and go back to my job tomorrow morning, that would be amazing.

I'd do fucking anything to have my normal, in-debt life back.

Across the bar, two men approached a woman who was more plastered than I was. I blinked a few times, trying to see straight, and squinted at the woman, unable to tell if she was just too drunk or if something had happened to her. Instead of pushing them away like I thought she would, she drew them closer and open-mouthed kissed both of them at the same time.

I slumped down in my seat, telling myself to forget her because I had my own damn problems to deal with, and asked for another drink. The bartender took my glass from me and poured me some water.

"I want another one," I said.

"You're too drunk," he said back.

After growling at him, I stumbled off the seat and stormed toward the exit. Marco kicked himself off the wall from across the room and followed me. Knowing that I wouldn't get far and wouldn't be able to lose him while I was *this* drunk, I pushed through the door and started my walk toward my brand-spanking-new apartment.

A night breeze blew gently over the city, and I shivered and peeked behind me to see Marco following. At least Cristian wasn't with him. I'd get to spend a couple of hours alone with Marco to convince him to kill for me, so Cristian would leave me the fuck alone. And I wanted Cristian to leave me alone more than anything.

18

STUMBLING INTO MY APARTMENT, I slammed the door right in Marco's face and stormed through the living room, straight to the file Cristian had given me earlier. I tore it in half, then in half again, then in half again. "Fuck you, Cristian."

I soaked the paper in water until I couldn't read the name anymore, and then I tossed it into the trash and resisted the urge to burn it.

Who the fuck does that man think he is, bossing me around and telling me to kill someone for him?

As if I want him or his trust.

Instead of waiting until the trash was full, I took the bag out of the can, tied it up, and stomped to the front door. Marco stood outside the door. He glanced up from his phone and arched a brow at the trash. "It's not even full."

I walked past him and toward the trash room, depositing the bag into the bucket and walking back out toward Marco, who had one foot stuck between the door and the doorframe so it wouldn't lock on me.

"We need to chat," I said to him, holding the door open so he'd walk into the room. When he didn't move, I arched a brow and pointed into the apartment. "Now. I don't have the damn patience today."

"Cristian will be home soon."

"This is Cristian's apartment?"

"He lives two floors up."

I crossed my arms over my chest and watched how his eyes flickered down for the slightest moment, and then I shrugged. "Well, I don't care what god-awful time of the night he's coming home. He's not coming here. Get in."

Great, Roxie. Order him around. That'll definitely get you brownie points with him.

Still, he didn't move.

So, I leaned against the doorframe, looked up at him through my lashes, and drew a finger up his chest. "Come on. Just for a minute. I need to ask you something in private."

This man must've been extremely loyal to Cristian or had some godly self-control because he didn't move an inch or even attempt to. Instead, he kept his cold, dead stare on me and—

I clutched my stomach, eyes widening. Dear Lord, I felt like I was about to—

Doubling over, I sprinted to the hallway to find the bathroom. Whatever the hell I'd drunk tonight was about to come up and spew out of my throat. Knocking open door after door, I tripped on my own two feet in the bathroom and smacked belly-first onto the ground, the feeling of needing to puke disappearing.

"Roxie, are you okay?" Marco said from the hall.

I decided that this might be the only damn way to trap him in here, so I groaned in response. "Can you help me?" I whined. "I hit my—"

Marco stood at the bathroom door and reached down to pick me up. "Fuck, Cristian is going to fucking murder me for this." He scooped me into his arms and walked down the hallway to the living room, setting me on the couch. "How much did you drink tonight, Roxie?"

I let my hands linger around his shoulders for a moment. "Too much."

The door flung open, and Cristian stepped into the room with his gun drawn. When he saw us by the couch, he swore at Marco and put his gun back into his waistband.

"What the fuck are you doing in here?" Cristian sneered at Marco. "I thought someone had fucking broken in."

Marco stood up straight. "Roxie fell."

Cristian looked at me and tilted his head, as if to say, *Oh, really?* Then, he pressed his lips together. "Out," Cristian said to Marco with his jaw clenched tight.

I wrapped my hand around Marco's tense bicep. "He's staying."

Cristian stared at me with intense brown eyes and clenched his jaw. "Out," he said, voice hard and tight with cruel rage, the same voice he had used on me countless times before tonight.

And without saying two words, Marco escaped through the front door and shut it behind him.

Heart pounding inside my chest, I nervously gulped and felt the blood drain from my face. Something about being alone with Cristian irked me. Maybe it was the way I felt about him or that stupid, sinister smirk plastered across his devilish face.

"Do you like making a fool of yourself?" Cristian asked me, stepping closer.

The alcohol had quickly worn off the damn second he stepped foot into the apartment and given me those cold, dark eyes.

"Do you like drinking until you can't walk and are stumbling out of my club like an idiot?"

I narrowed my eyes at him, hopped up, and poked him in the chest. "Don't talk down to me. I just watched my fiancé die, witnessed a man get tortured, and lost my job because of you. If I want to get hammered just one night, then I will. You don't fucking own me."

Cristian chuckled menacingly and took another step toward me, looming over me. "*Principessa,* do you need a reminder? I thought you would've already gotten it through that pretty little head of yours that I own everything around here. The apartment, your bodyguard, everyone at my club." He brushed a finger against my cheek and tucked some hair behind my ear, leaning close. "Yet my most valuable possession is you."

Overcome with anger, I thrust my hands against his chest to push him away. He caught them and held them against his taut chest, stepping between my legs and grinding his hard cock against me. "Ask me why you're my most valuable. I dare you."

My heart raced in my chest, and I gulped nervously. "Why, Cristian?"

"Because I'm going to make you the Ricci family's cruelest, most heartless killer, Manhattan's most wanted mob member, and"—he captured my earlobe between his teeth and tugged on it gently—"my wife one day."

19

roxie

"YOUR WIFE?" I whispered, tasting the title on my tongue.

Cristian wasn't suggesting, wasn't asking, and wasn't even demanding. He was telling me that, one day, I would be his wife, whether I wanted to be or not. I would be married to the Manhattan devil, would learn to kill innocent people, and would relish in the punishment that Cristian served.

Heat crawled up my neck, wrapped around my throat, and suffocated me.

If I'd thought I would ever be able to get out of this situation, I was wrong. The moment that Ben had stolen money from the Mafia boss, my fate had been sealed. I had been his for longer than I'd ever thought I was.

"Why?" I asked, my voice trembling.

Fear ran through every one of my veins, down my spine, into my bones, paralyzing me. I couldn't understand why he wanted me. He could have anyone in the entire world, but … me?

"Why me? Why are you doing this to me?"

Just a couple days ago, I had been engaged to Ben. We were supposed to be married. We were supposed to spend the rest of our lives together. Yet, within such a short time, everything had turned on its head.

"You haven't figured it out yet, *principessa*?" Cristian asked, brow furrowed in an angry stare. He drew his tongue across his bottom lip, looked down at me with such pain, and stepped away. "Of course you haven't."

My eyes widened slightly at his sudden bitterness. With tense shoulders, he turned away and headed to one of the many drawers in the kitchen. God, this man was literally the definition of bipolar. One minute, he wanted me to marry him, and then the next, he was storming away from me and pulling out a gu—

"Why is there a fucking gun in the kitchen?!" I asked. I backed up slowly, my heart pounding hard inside my chest. The backs of my legs hit the edge of the couch. "And why did you take it out?"

Cristian shut the counter drawer and ran his finger along the barrel of the gun. "This is one of my sister's guns. I stole it from her for you to have." He walked over to me and held out the gun for me to take. "It will do for now until I can get one made for you."

I glared down at the piece of metal that had been built for the sole purpose of killing.

"Take the fucking gun, Roxie," Cristian said, anger laced in every one of his words.

"No."

"Don't fucking test me right now. I'm not in the mood."

"I'm not touching that fucking thing. I have no use for it. I'm not killing that man."

Cristian growled and wrapped his hand around the grip. "You will use it, and when you do, you need to know how to use it," he said to me.

He started pointing to different parts of the gun, naming them and telling me what they did.

While I didn't want to know a thing about it, I decided to pay attention to him for once. If I was going to kill anyone, it would be Cristian Ricci. Every Manhattan cop who had been looking for him and every rival mobster who wanted to kill him would be disappointed because I would be the one to end this man's life.

But I needed to know how to use a gun to kill him.

When he finished, he placed the gun down on the sidetable next to me. He stared at me for a few moments, then tore his gaze away. "I don't want you touching Marco ever again. You will not invite him into your house. You will not use him for your dirty work. You will not think about him." He clenched his jaw and turned away, walking toward the door. "You will kill who I ask you to kill yourself."

"No," I said, my voice trembling. I clasped the gun in a shaky hand, lifted it, and pointed it directly at the back of his head. Sick of trembling and crying and seeming weak, I shook my head and glared at his back. "I'm not fucking killing an innocent man, but I'll kill a guilty one."

Cristian turned around, eyes widening slightly when he saw the gun pointed at him, but he quickly recollected himself and straightened out his back, staring intensely at me with those devilish brown eyes. "Do it, *principessa*." He stepped closer to me. "You want to kill me? Put a bullet straight through my head?" He moved even closer, grabbed the barrel of the gun, and pressed it against his forehead. "Fucking do it."

I could kill the man if I wanted to. I could end this all for good, end all the pain and suffering of hundreds of families across New York, get revenge for my grandfather, who had been tortured by the Ricci family and so traumatized that he refused to speak to any of his family anymore.

"Do it," Cristian taunted me.

My fingers trembled against the trigger.

"What are you waiting for?"

After glaring at him for a few more moments, I threw the gun onto the couch. "Fuck you."

Cristian shook his head. "You have a lot to fucking learn, *principessa*. The next time you aim that gun at me, you'd better pull the trigger, or I'll fucking teach you to obey. I've waited too fucking long for you."

I tore my gaze away from him and glared down at my feet. What the hell did he mean that he waited for so long to be with me? I had just met him a couple days ago, and he already wanted to *marry* me?

"Stay away from anybody you don't know," Cristian said over his shoulder while walking to the door. "Now that you're part of the Ricci family, you have a target on your back, *principessa*. Everyone will want a piece of you. Don't be afraid to use that gun."

20

cristian

"YOUR TOTAL IS four thousand three hundred fifty-six dollars," the associate said the next day, folding all the clothes I'd bought for Roxie and placing them in three separate black bags. After I handed her my card, she finished ringing me out and waved me off. "Next time, bring her with you, so we can get her measurements."

I grabbed the bags and walked out of the store to find Chiara waiting for me at the exit.

"What'd you get the woman who hates you the most?" she asked me with a smirk. She took a peek in the bags and scrunched her nose. "God, you have bad taste. Next time, just give Roxie your black card, and I'll take her out."

"You don't think she'll like it?"

Chiara arched a brow. "It's too prissy for her. With all her tattoos and that dyed hair, Roxie is spunky. She stands out. She's not going to want to dress in some old-lady-looking clothes. These might help her fit in with the other girls in the family, but it's not her."

"You have anything else to say?" I asked, feeling on edge ever since I'd left her this morning.

She crossed her arms. "You have your hands full with her."

"Don't remind me," I said through clenched teeth.

After last night, that was fucking clear. That woman had dared to hold a gun—one that she'd sworn she didn't want to use—right to my head. Nobody—*nobody*—had fucking dared to do that before. Not even Alessa, my crazy ex-fling.

"Did you bring me what I'd asked for?" I asked Chiara.

She opened her oversize purse and showed me the gun inside of it. "Personalized for Roxie. I even got her initials etched on the grip, just like mine. Do you think she'll like it?" Chiara asked, overly excited about Roxie.

But I didn't blame her. She didn't really have any other females in her family she could trust. The majority of her family had left the business after she killed her father for taking part in the child trafficking ring.

"She'll like it," I lied.

She hated guns.

"When you get back from Boston after dealing with some of your family, tell Roxie that we're going out shopping and having a girls' day. I won't take no for an answer because that girl needs friends."

My phone buzzed in my pocket.

Piero: Marco is at the house.

"I have to go," I said, stuffing my phone into my pocket and opening my car door.

"Tell Roxie I said hi!" Chiara said, shutting the door.

As soon as the door closed, I stepped on the gas and sped toward the house. I had been waiting to see Marco all fucking day.

When I made it to the house, I walked down the steps to the dungeon. Charlie groaned from the X-styled cross I had tied him to as I walked past him, but I ignored his ass and continued until I came face-to-face with Marco in the other room.

"Charlie acting up again?" Marco asked.

"I told you to guard her, not to fucking touch her."

Marco widened his eyes. "This is about Roxie?" He scoffed. "Are you ser—"

I slammed my fist into the side of Marco's face and relished in how quickly his skin turned black and blue. "Don't fucking test me, Marco. You fucking know better than that."

Marco stumbled down, stared up at me, and shook his head. "You told me to fuck her. I thought she was another one of the family who—"

Before he finished, I hit him again. "She's not one of the family whores."

"I didn't fucking know she actually meant something to you."

"You knew. You just didn't fucking care."

Marco spat some blood on the concrete floor of the dungeon. "What the fuck do you want me to say to you? I didn't fucking know. If you had wanted to keep her to yourself, you should've."

"Or I shouldn't trust fuckheads like *you*." I kneeled down to his level and grasped his jaw. "You see anyone else who fucked her the other night try to touch her again? Huh?" I slapped him across the face. "Did anyone else decide to walk into her apartment and touch her?"

"She fell," he said through clenched teeth.

"You didn't answer my fucking question."

"No."

"Right. *Nobody* touched her, except *you*." I pushed him away and stepped back before I lost it and killed him right here and now. "Let this be a fucking warning, Marco. Touch her again, and I'll kill you."

21

roxie

INSTEAD OF AN ALARM blaring in my ear, I woke up to sunlight warming my face. As I blinked my eyes open, I turned onto my side and stared out of my floor-to-ceiling bedroom windows. Not having work was almost a relief. Maybe I could get away with not having to kill that man at all.

If I could wake up like this every day, I'd be set.

When I decided to finally drag myself out of bed, I turned onto my back and noticed three black bags on the edge of my bed. I shuffled to the headboard and eyed them for a couple of moments. Cristian had been here, inside my bedroom, to give me these while I slept this morning. It had to have been him because Cristian wouldn't let Marco come near me, not after last night.

The way he had told me not to touch Marco with such cruelty made it seem like he was almost possessive. But he had let his men take me so easily the other day. Again, another Cristian paradox that I would never understand.

After I got out of the shower, looked through all the old-woman clothes from Barneys, and found *one damn dress* that I liked, I walked out the apartment door, hoping to find Marco. Yet there was a man I had never seen before standing outside my door with dark sunglasses and dressed in a black suit.

"Roxie?" he asked me.

I eyed him. "Who are you?"

"Your bodyguard for the day."

I balled my hands into fists. "Where is Marco?"

Instead of answering me, he ignored my question completely. "Cristian is at his club, working."

———

"You're wearing the clothes I bought you," Cristian said to me when I arrived, crossing his arms over his chest and leaning back in his chair. Looking me up and down, he curled his lips into the smallest of smirks. "I thought you'd fill these out quite nicely."

I glared at him. "It's not like I had much of a choice. You won't bring me back to my old apartment. I have to fit into these grossly expensive clothes that aren't even worth the price tag."

"You can't politely accept anything, can you?"

"No, I can't. Why are you doing this?"

"Doing what?"

"Being nice to me? Buying me clothes? Telling me you want to marry me?"

An unreadable expression crossed his face. He grimaced and stood, walking over to me and grasping my chin in his rough hand. He pulled it to one side and then the other, as if he was searching my face for something. Eventually, he frowned and shook his head.

"You really don't remember me, do you?" he asked, sadness laced in his words.

I shoved my hands against his chest and forced him back a few inches. Every time he got this close, I … I fucking hated it. It made me feel things I should never ever feel for him. And it irked me to no end.

"What the hell are you talking about?" I asked, so desperately confused.

Cristian cleared his throat and walked back behind his desk. "Go."

"Fine." I turned on my heel and walked right out of the room, bumping into Marco.

Though he was supposed to be my bodyguard, it was the first time I had seen him today. And to say he looked bad was an understatement. He stepped away from me with a nasty black bruise under his eye and a busted lip.

Did Cristian do that to him?

"Marco," I said loud enough for Cristian to hear, "come have a drink with me."

It probably wasn't the best idea for me to get drunk here for the second day in a row or to even be around booze after watching what I had for the past few days. Yet I planned to stay sober and get Cristian angry enough to stop being an annoying asshole who talked in phrases that didn't make sense.

"Marco," Cristian growled from the office.

Marco went to step beside me, but I grabbed his wrist and brushed my thumb over the bruise on his face.

"What happened to you?" I asked, brow furrowed, even though I knew exactly what had happened to him. "Walk me home, and I'll get you some ice."

To my surprise, Marco actually didn't refuse as quickly as I'd thought he would.

He grabbed my wrist and pulled my hand off his face. "You're going to get me killed, Roxie," he said so quietly that Cristian wouldn't be able to hear.

"You don't want me to take care of your wounds?" I inched closer to him. Though Cristian might've been the boss of this family, I found Marco to be one of the most attractive Riccis here. I stood on my toes, loving the feeling of being so small beside him, and brushed my lips against his jaw. "Nurse you back to health?"

Marco glanced down at me, gaze traveling from my eyes to my lips, then back up.

"Marco," Cristian sneered, grabbing him by the collar and

yanking him inside the room. He turned to me. "Watch yourself, *principessa.* I know you're trying to get on my fucking nerves for some ungodly reason. You piss me off one more fucking time, and it won't be Marco I take it out on."

"Is that supposed to be a threat?" I asked, arching a brow.

He snatched me by the throat and pulled me closer. "It's a fucking promise, Roxie."

When he pushed me away, I growled at him and stormed down the hallway toward the bar. The bartender poured me a white sangria and placed it in front of me. I sipped it slowly, not wanting to get drunk off this thing tonight and make a complete fool out of myself again.

A petite woman with huge breasts jumped onto the seat next to me. "Hi, Roxie."

I glanced over at her and arched a brow. "Do I know you?"

"No, but Cristian does," she said.

Instead of giving this girl another moment of my time, I turned back to the bar and glanced over at a couple of guys being handsy with a girl who looked beyond uncomfortable. One of the men leaned closer while the girl laughed awkwardly and gave a tense smile.

Biting my lip, I itched to go over there and punch the man right in the nose. I had so much anger pent-up inside me that it was hard to think straight. I wanted to take it out on someone, and apparently, taking it out on Cristian would be a bad idea on my part. And besides, no girl should ever feel *that* uncomfortable.

After waving the bartender over, I leaned over the bar. "Watch that girl, please."

The bitch who knew Cristian grabbed my arm and yanked me back. "Did you hear anything that I just said to you?" she sneered at me, her fake hot-pink nails digging into my forearm and definitely leaving little marks.

"Excuse me?" I asked, ready to fucking snap. "Take your hand off me before I do it myself."

"Stay away from Cr—"

"What the fuck are you doing here, Alessa?" Cristian asked, pulling me off the barstool and behind him. "I told you that you weren't welcome here unless you were with my sister. Now, get out of my club, or you will be escorted out."

Alessa jumped off the stool and went to trail her nasty fingers up Cristian's abdomen, but Cristian caught her wrist.

"Out. Now," he said through clenched teeth.

Alessa hummed to herself, crossed her arms over her chest, and stormed out of the club.

"Who was that?" I asked.

"Nobody you need to worry about."

"I think I do," I said. "She left claw marks in my forearm."

"I'll take care of her. Now, come with me and don't make this difficult," Cristian said, grabbing my hand.

I yanked my hand away from his, held it to my chest, and reluctantly followed after the man I hated the most. We walked all the way down the hallway to his office, but instead of slipping inside of it, we continued toward the back door.

Marco opened the door for us. I walked out into the back alley and eyed the sleek black car that was owned by none other than Cristian. Cristian opened the passenger door for me and gestured for me to get into the car.

"No questions," Cristian said before I could speak. "Get in."

I growled to myself and slid into the passenger seat. After he got into the car with me, I glanced over at him, brow furrowed.

"Where are we going?" I asked him despite him telling me not to.

He tightened his hand around the steering wheel. "Boston."

22

cristian

INSTEAD OF TALKING TO ME, Roxie had crossed her arms over her chest and glared out the window for the entire four-hour drive to Boston. She didn't ask to stop or look over at me or uncross her arms once.

When I pulled up to the curb of Mickey's house, she finally glanced at me. The dawn sun flooded into the car and hit her brown eyes, making them a sea of gold.

She uncrossed her arms and sat up. "What are we doing here?"

"Same thing we did to Charlie."

All the blood drained from her rosy cheeks. "Why?" she asked me, voice barely above a whisper.

She turned in my direction, and I couldn't tell if she was truly intrigued or if she was terrified by the mere thought of torturing someone else.

Instead of sugarcoating this for her, like I had with any of my previous girlfriends, I undid my seat belt and pulled the keys out of the car. "Because he groomed and raped a thirteen-year-old girl. And to make matters worse than fucking that, he did it in one of my restaurants."

She widened her eyes and grasped her seat belt until her knuckles turned white. "Are you serious?" she asked. Tears welled up in her eyes. "Did he really do that to someone?"

"Yes."

"Can I stay here?" she asked.

"No. If you're going to be my wife one day, you're going to watch *everything* I do."

She tore her gaze away from me as soon as the word *wife* left my mouth and opened her door. I followed after her and walked to the front door, knocking twice on it with the side of my fist and waiting not so patiently for him.

Dressed in nothing but a barely closed robe and some glasses, Mickey answered the door. When he noticed it was me, he stood up straight and widened his eyes. "Cristian. I-I didn't expect—"

I stepped into his house without an invitation and waited for Roxie to come in before I shut the door. Mickey stepped back to create distance between us, but I moved closer to him, feeling the rage seep into my veins.

Instead of giving him a chance to explain himself, like I had promised myself I would do, I punched him straight in the jaw and listened to his glasses crack into two pieces. He stumbled back into a closet and nearly took the door off its hinges.

"Cristian," he got out. "Wh-what was that—"

"You know exactly what it was for," I said, grabbing him by the neck, pulling him out of the closet, and pinning him to the wall. My fingers dug into his neck until the skin turned pink. "You must have known that this was coming for months now. But you couldn't seem to keep your hands off that girl, could you?"

He widened his eyes even more and grabbed my wrist. "Cristian, you should be focused on your shipments. Not worrying about stupid little shit like this in the family. There are far more important—"

I slammed my other fist into his jaw and watched his eyes roll to the back of his head. When he came back to consciousness, I let my nails dig into the sides of his neck so hard that I drew blood. He spat at me, and I spat right back.

"I stay out of your business. Why do you even fucking care about what I do?"

"Because it's wrong."

He let out a lifeless chuckle. "And racketeering, dealing drugs, and murder aren't?"

I blew out a deep breath. Child trafficking or sex with a minor was more than just wrong. I had witnessed what it could do to a person. I dropped my hand from his throat and glanced over at Roxie, letting my eyes linger for a moment longer than they should've.

"Do you want to do the honors?" I asked her.

She scrunched her nose and stepped away from me, crossing her arms over her chest. I pulled out a knife and slid it right across Mickey's neck, letting his blood drip all over my hands. He grasped his throat to try to stop the blood and doubled over onto his knees.

Someone screamed at the top of their lungs, and I glanced toward the stairs to see Mickey's wife.

"C-C-Cristian. Wh-what did you do?" she asked me, running down the stairs and crouching next to her husband. She placed her hands on his neck to stop the blood.

"If I find out you were in on this the entire time, you're next," I sneered at her.

I washed my hands off in the kitchen sink, grabbed Roxie's hand, and pulled her out the door and away from the hysterical woman, doubled over her disgusting husband.

Roxie stayed silent the entire ride to the hotel, pressing her lips together and staring wide-eyed through the windshield. After fifteen minutes of silence, she parted her plum-colored lips. "Why didn't you torture him, like you had with Charlie?"

Not expecting her question, I tightened my grip on the steering wheel. I'd expected her to shout at me for killing him or cry or ask me what the hell she was here for yet again. But she just glanced over at me with a furrowed brow.

"I don't have an answer for you," I said honestly. "I didn't want to deal with him, especially when I don't live in Boston. He's now an example for all the Ricci family members here—don't fuck with me, or I'll kill you."

After pulling up to the hotel, I led Roxie to the foyer, took the keys from the front desk, and led her to the elevator. To my surprise, Roxie let me intertwine my fingers with hers as I led her to the top floor, which was all ours.

I didn't want this weekend to be all about Mickey. He had been taken care of already.

This weekend was for us.

I pushed the door to our room open and gestured for Roxie to walk in before me.

"One bed?" She crossed her arms over her chest. "You got us a room with one bed?"

I took off my suit jacket and undid my tie, glancing from the bed over to her with hungry eyes. She shifted from foot to foot and stared at me. After tugging off my tie, I tossed it onto the bed and grabbed a bottle of sambuca from the counter.

"Have a drink, *principessa*, and relax. It's for one night."

"You have the money to get us two rooms."

"I do, but I won't," I said, words coming out sharp, hard, and final. "You're sleeping in that bed with me tonight."

I would finally have her in my arms tonight after years of hoping, wishing, and imagining it.

Roxie would be mine tonight.

23

roxie

ONE DRINK TURNED into two drinks, and by three drinks, I was feeling good. *Too* good actually. I couldn't quite understand why I wasn't soaking up this lifestyle that Cristian was so generously offering me. Was I being hard on him for no reason at all?

After putting down my glass, I glanced over at him sitting on the balcony and talking to someone on the phone. From the way he had so savagely tortured that man earlier—blood dripping down his hands, muscles swollen underneath his shirt, eyes as dark as the deepest pits of hell—he had made me feel things that a woman like me *should never* feel for a devil like him.

I took another sip. God, when I drank, I wanted one of two things: to fight or to fuck.

Now, I wanted a bit of both.

I stormed to the balcony, pulled the phone out of his hand, and shut it off. Cristian glared up at me and snatched his phone away from me, standing up to his full height and looking down at me.

"What's your problem today? I said, drink to relax, not to fucking fight me."

"We need to talk, Cristian," I said through clenched teeth,

glaring up at him. "I want to be brought home. I didn't want to even come to Boston with you, didn't want to watch you kill someone, and especially didn't want to share a bed with you!"

To my surprise, Cristian kept himself composed. "Get yourself another drink and go to sleep."

Wanting a better response, I thrust my hands against his chest. "No. I want to go home," I said, pushing him even harder. "Take me the fuck home now. I don't want to spend a second more here." Another hard shove into the railing.

"Stop shoving me," he said, clenching his jaw.

To set him off, I pushed him again. "I fucking hate yo—"

Cristian grabbed my wrists in one of his hands, turned us around so I was forced against the railing, and pressed himself against me. With his face inches from mine, I could taste the sambuca on his lips. He had been out here, drinking, since we had checked into the hotel for the night, just as I had.

"Don't. Fucking. Push me."

"Or what?" I asked, tilting my head up at him. "What are you *really* going to do about it, Cristian?"

He grabbed my chin and shoved me harder against the railing, fingers digging into my skin. After stepping closer to me, he pressed his lips against mine and kissed me hard. He slipped his hands around my body and tugged me toward him, his breath against my lips. Tearing the buttons right off my shirt, ripping off my bra, kissing down my neck, Cristian turned me around on the balcony and stuck his hand into my pants.

"Fuuuck, *principessa*," he murmured into my ear. "So fucking wet for me."

I pushed my hips back against his and felt his lips move down the side of my neck and press against my shoulder.

After rubbing myself against him some more, feeling his hard cock against my backside, I grasped the railing and moaned louder than I should've. Though we had the entire top floor to ourselves, there were people under us.

Nothing about it was soft or gentle as he thrust his fingers into me and curled them over and over to massage my G-spot until I doubled over and screamed out his name. He sucked on the skin on my neck, no doubt leaving blotchy red marks, as if he was claiming me with them.

I went to turn around, to kneel for him even, just wanting to have his huge cock in my mouth. I wanted him to use my body, to ram himself into my throat, to make himself feel good with me. But he moved closer, wrapped his arm around my neck, making it hard for me to breathe, and forced me to arch my back.

"You're not going anywhere," he murmured into my neck, undoing his belt, pulling himself out, and rubbing his hard cock against me. "I'm going to make your pussy a sopping mess and then ruin it again and again and again, Roxie," he said, voice slurred. He pushed the head of his cock against my pussy and then thrust himself all the way inside of me. "All night long, you're going to be screaming for me."

Lightly biting down on my jaw, Cristian pounded into me. Every time he thrust into me, my tits bounced against the railing, my nipples hardening against the slight wind.

He slapped one of my tits, wrapped his arm harder around my neck, and pulled me off the railing. He rammed himself into me as he walked toward the chair. I stumbled onto it on my hands and knees and looked back at him, brow furrowing.

Like a wild, savage, ruthless animal, Cristian grasped my hips and continued to ruin me. His hair flopped against his forehead, thick strands sticking to the sweat there. He pushed three fingers into my mouth and forced me to suck on them.

Pressure built up in my core. I curled my fingers into the cushion and stared back at him with wide eyes as spit dripped down my chin and onto the chair. I thrust a hand between my legs and rubbed my clit, driving myself higher and higher and tightening around him.

"*Principessa*, if you keep tightening your pussy like that ..." Cristian got out through raspy breaths. "You're going to make me come deep in your—" He suddenly tensed, stilled, and groaned out loud. "Fuck." After a couple of moments, he pumped slowly into me.

Close to the edge of losing control, I squeezed my eyes closed and focused on every inch of him as he pulled out of me.

He grasped my jaw. "Push my cum out, *principessa*," he said as he grabbed a handful of my ass in his hand. He slipped his other arm around my waist and slowly rubbed my clit, sending me higher and higher. "I want you to see how much of me is inside of you."

I clenched myself harder as his fingers moved around my clit. When the first of his cum dripped out of me and onto the cushion, I found myself trembling. Wave after wave of pleasure rushed through me as more of his cum dripped, creating a small puddle.

After a few moments, Cristian groaned. "*Principessa*," he murmured, "let me take a picture of this pussy, creamed with my cum."

"A ... a picture?" I whispered, tightening at the thought. More of his cum dribbled out.

He softly rubbed a hand against my ass. "You're so fucking sexy like this, Roxie. Let me take a picture, so I can jack off to it while I work," he said, running his thumb down my lips.

The pressure started to rise in my core again. Deep down, I knew it was a bad idea to let Cristian have a naked picture of me on his phone, but I couldn't stop my drunk ass from nodding like a fool.

Cristian grabbed his phone from the table and opened his camera. "Look back at me, Roxie."

I gulped and looked back, gently biting my lip. This was wrong —so fucking wrong—but I couldn't help but tighten more. "Put yourself back inside me," I said, needing him so fucking bad.

"Keep begging for it. Keep fucking begging," Cristian said, his phone still pointed at me. He rubbed his cock against my creamed pussy. "You're making me hard again, baby."

"Cristian, don't do this. Please, give it to me. Please, fuck me again."

Cristian tossed the phone onto the table, wrapped his arms

around my waist, and carried me to the bed, crawling onto it with me. "I said that I would fuck you all night long, Roxie. I plan to keep my word."

24

roxie

WITH DISHEVELED SEX hair and his bare back covered in all sorts of scars from bullet and knife wounds, Cristian lay next to me, sleeping. Moonlight flooded in through the sheer white curtains of the penthouse, making his olive skin glow. And while I wanted to tear my gaze away from him, I couldn't.

After we'd had sex for the first time alone, it had taken *everything* to convince myself that I didn't like it and could live without the man. I had been staring up at the ceiling for hours now, trying so desperately to leave.

It was my chance to run and escape Cristian for good. We were in Boston, a city that he wasn't as familiar with compared to New York. If I ran out of this hotel room, down the street, and slipped into a stall in a women's restroom in one of the many Boston bars, he would never find me.

My heart pounded in my chest, and I gently pulled the blankets off me and quietly scooched to the edge of the bed. The springs in the mattress creaked, and I cursed to myself for making a sound. I paused, made sure Cristian's eyes were still closed, and continued moving as quietly as possible.

Just when I was about to stand, Cristian grabbed my wrist and yanked me back down.

"Where are you going?" he asked, opening one eye to look at me. "You're not leaving."

"I need some fresh air," I lied.

"There's a balcony," Cristian said, moving up the bed and leaning against the headboard with his big arms crossed over his chest. He gestured to the sliding glass door and waited *patiently* for me to respond.

I shot up from the bed, told myself that I might as well run now while he was naked under the sheets, and sprinted toward the door. Why was I still running away from him? Other than hating the man for ruining my life, something about him reminded me of distant memories that I couldn't quite remember completely, but I did feel as if they were haunting and gave me chills.

Before I could make it to the door, Cristian wrapped his arms around my waist from behind, shoved me against the wall, and pressed his body against me. "How many fucking times do I have to say it? You're not leaving," he growled into my ear. "I've waited too fucking long for you."

"You say that like you fucking know me," I sneered through my teeth. I tried to push myself off the wall and away from him, but he pressed harder against me. "I just want to leave. I never asked for this life. Why are you doing this to me? You've been acting like you know me for days now."

To my surprise, Cristian pushed himself off me, stormed to his wallet, and opened it up. "You want to go out into the city alone at night?" he asked me, fumbling through his wallet. "Go. Do whatever the fuck you need to do, but be fucking back by morning, or I'll find you and drag you back to Manhattan myself."

He turned the wallet upside down, opened the pockets up, and let about twenty hundred-dollar bills fall out of it along with a white sheet of paper that couldn't be bigger than a credit card. I glanced down at all the money with my brow furrowed and shook my head.

This man flipped through a variety of emotions, all within a few moments. Horny. Angry. Content and composed. Furious and cruel. It was like being a damn contestant on the *Wheel of Fortune* and wondering which card the dial would land on.

After slapping his wallet on the counter, pouring himself a glass of alcohol, and walking over to the sliding glass door, he stepped out onto the balcony in nothing but a pair of underwear and slammed the door behind him.

Without saying a word, I kneeled and gathered all the cash. Was I going to take it and run? No. I didn't want any more of his damn money. That was what had gotten Ben into this mess. But was the thought of escaping his wrath and not having to walk on eggshells around him anymore tempting? Hell fucking yes.

I shoved every single dollar back into his wallet and picked up the white sheet of paper, turning it around to see that it wasn't a sheet of paper after all. On one side was a date—*December 14, 1994*. I turned the sheet over to see a picture of two young kids, an old man, and someone who looked almost exactly like Cristian at a Christmas party.

My chest tightened, throat drying. One of those kids was me, sitting on my grandfather's lap, and next to …

My heart dropped. "No," I whispered, shaking my head.

This didn't make sense. If this was me, Cristian, my grandfather, and Cristian's grandfather … it didn't make sense at all. My grandfather had hated Cristian's grandfather and the entire Ricci family for as long as I could remember.

Grandpa had his hands around my waist, smiling as he looked down at me with those old, teary blue eyes, the sunspots apparent on his bald head. All I could remember was a grumpy man who was out in his garage all the time. Sometimes, he'd even take me into the garage to help him, but he had never looked *this* happy.

Bits and pieces of memories came flooding back into my mind of going over to my grandparents' house and playing with a boy when I was younger. But … Cristian? I couldn't seem to remember it was him. Come to think of it … I couldn't remember much of spending time at Grandma and Grandpa's house.

What did we do most of those days?

After clutching the picture in my hand, I stormed over to the balcony, ripped open the glass door, and shoved the picture against Cristian's chest. "Why the hell do you have this?" I asked him, something tightening in the pit of my stomach.

More suppressed memories continued to whiz through my mind as tears welled up in my eyes. Something wasn't right. Something was making me feel disgusted, sick even. I wanted to double over on the balcony and puke my dinner up.

Cristian took the picture from me, registered what I had seen, and stood up. "Do you remember me now?" he asked suddenly.

I clutched on to the railing until my knuckles turned white, yet he stepped closer.

"Do you remember all those nights my grandfather brought me over and we'd play together? All those nights we threw rocks down by the river and stuck our toes in the water and—"

"And we would hang out with Willy," I continued in a breath, feeling my chest tighten more every second that passed.

"Willy," Cristian said lifelessly. "You always loved him, didn't you?"

"Cristian … I-I barely remember him," I whispered. Because I could barely remember him at all, just his name. Every memory of mine before the age of five seemed to be such a blur. It was as if I had purposefully tried to block them all out for some reason.

Cristian stepped toward me, alcohol heavy on his breath. "Willy fucking loved you. You'd choose to play with him over and over again. I could never fucking have you, Roxie. Never. So, you want to know what I did?"

I gulped and shook my head. I didn't want to know.

"I killed him."

"You're fucking insane," I whispered, stepping back even further until my back hit the other side of the railing. "Insane. You're making this all up. It's a lie. My grandfather *hated* your family. He'd never smile in a picture with your grandfather."

"My grandfather and your grandfather were business partners," Cristian said to me.

I shook my head and crossed my arms over my chest to protect myself. Pain festered inside of me at the even deeper bottled-up memories that were slowly starting to seep into my brain. "No. You're lying. My grandfather hated him."

A look of hurt and sorrow crossed Cristian's face for a moment. He went to grab my hand, but I pulled myself away from him and stared into his eyes, waiting for him to spew another lie so I could shoot it down. I didn't want to remember. My entire body was telling me to run away now, so I couldn't feel how I'd felt all those years ago. However that had felt.

"They stopped business when my grandfather found out what your grandfather had been doing to you."

"Doing to me?" I asked, my voice somehow even smaller than it had been.

"I'm not going to say it aloud, Roxie. You know. You've just suppressed it."

Tears welled up in my eyes as the memories burst through my head. I doubled over and curled up into a ball.

No … no. I didn't want to believe it. I didn't want to think about it. I didn't want to even feel it. But all I could seem to feel now was Grandpa's hands all over my body in places that they should never have been.

25

cristian

WITH GLOSSY EYES and flushed cheeks, Roxie continued to shake her head, as if she didn't believe it or didn't *want* to believe it. I'd never wanted to be the one to bring back those old memories, but she didn't understand how much killing fuckers like her grandfather meant to me.

What he had done to her was fucking repulsive, disgusting, and sickening.

It'd screwed her up for fucking years and would continue to screw with her head.

"I'm doing this to protect you and any other fucking child from men like your grandfather," I said as tears slid down her cheeks. "Pick yourself up. Stop crying. Face reality. What happened to you is happening to hundreds of other fucking kids, Roxie. That's why I kill them, not because I fucking want to, but because they deserve it."

I didn't know where I was going with it, but I had to fucking get it out. For years, I had shielded myself away from her. For weeks, I had tried to be nice. The real, heartless Cristian was here now, and I couldn't hold him back any longer. He wanted Roxie to be safe, to be his, and he wouldn't let her go this time.

She slapped me hard across the face, then slammed her hands against my chest. "You can't even be quiet for a fucking moment as I try to process everything you've told me." She pushed me back. "I just learned that my grandfather molested me, and all you can talk about is yourself." She pushed me harder until I was pressed against the railing, and then she smashed the side of her fist against my chest. "I hate you. I—" More tears streamed down her face, faster than they had before. "I hate you." She shook her head and suddenly doubled over into me, face buried against my chest.

Out of instinct, I wrapped my arms around her to hold her up. If this were any other situation, I would've let her drop because intimate contact like this wasn't my forte. Sure, I could fuck Roxie every night of the week … but having her cry tears in my arms, just comforting *any* girl, wasn't my strong suit.

I wanted to tell her that it would all be okay, but it wouldn't.

I would try hard to make it okay, to make this world better for her, but it would never be the same. Her family had ruined that a long time ago when they let her grandfather do that to her. If Roxie ever wanted me to, I'd kill them for her too. Anything to make her happy and make her mine.

"Why?" She sobbed and clutched on to me. "Why did he do that to me?"

I wrapped my arms around her harder and pulled her to my chest. I didn't have an answer for her. I didn't know what had gone through his sick mind to ever think it was acceptable to do that to a child.

"Answer me!" she shouted, though I knew her anger wasn't really directed at me.

Instead of answering her, I held her tighter and stroked her hair, letting her cry into my chest and get it all out. After tonight, she wouldn't be over it. This shit would haunt her for the rest of her life.

"Roxie," I said, scooping her into my arms.

I walked with her over to the bed and lay down in it with her in my arms. She shifted in the bed until her head was against my scarred chest and clutched on to my waist.

I rubbed small circles on her shoulder. "Don't give that man any of your tears. He doesn't deserve it. Nobody like that does."

I lay with her for hours, stroking her hair and hoping she'd fall asleep and get some rest. But she continued to twist and turn and grumble and cry to herself. She curled up into my chest like I'd always wanted her to do, but not like this.

After a few more moments, she sat up and looked down at me. I pushed some more tears off her cheeks and grasped her jaw, letting her lean into me.

She gave me a half-smile—a weak and trying half-smile—then frowned. "That's why you hate people like that?" she asked. "Because of what my grandfather did to me?"

"Yes."

"I saw you torture Charlie," she said, shaking her head. "It's fun to you."

I pressed my lips together and swallowed hard, boiling heat crawling up my neck. I shook my head. "It's not fun. It's what needs to be done. I'd do that to anyone who tried to hurt you again. I'll protect you."

While her facial features softened just a bit, she shoved me away and wiped the tears from her cheeks. "I don't need your protection," she sneered, yanking the blankets toward her and moving to the other side of the bed. "I'm not that little girl anymore. One who needs you to fight off the bad guys for me. I'm perfectly capable of doing that myself now."

"There isn't any shame in—"

"Stop!" she said, pulling the blankets over her head. "Stop. It is shameful. Everything that has ever happened to me is shameful. My own grandfather abused me for years, and I forgot about it. *I fucking forgot about it,* Cristian." She glanced away. "Stop trying to be my savior."

I moved closer to her and placed my hand on her hip, but she quickly pushed it away.

"I don't need you. I-I can't need you," she whispered. "Stop being nice to me. I'm supposed to hate you."

26

roxie

I STABBED my pancakes with a fork, just like I wanted to stab my grandfather's cold, dead heart. All last night, I couldn't sleep because of him. I'd tossed and turned in the bed, throwing the sheets off me and then curling up into them. All those evil memories of my childhood haunted me. They had been stowed away for so long, just waiting for the day I unleashed them. Now, they were here, and they weren't leaving.

Every place my grandfather had trailed his fingers, every curve, every crevice, every hole ...

I felt it. I fucking felt it.

Grandma and my parents must've known what was happening, yet they had treated him like he had never touched me a day in his life, told stories about him after he died, like he was some sort of god. But that man had been nothing more than a cruel bastard who didn't deserve to live.

It scared me to think that because that was how Cristian felt. And that was what had led Cristian to become the cold-blooded killer he was today. Was that how I was bound to end up? Killing people until my life ends, not caring for the families I was ruining?

The waiter at the restaurant we were at walked over to our table with a huge grin and refilled my glass of water. "How's everything tasting? Anything else I can do for you, miss?"

"You can leave," Cristian said quickly before I could answer, a jealous look on his face.

He'd even irked me, too, trying to be all cute and nice to me last night. It wasn't who Cristian was, yet part of me … fucking loved it. I wanted to curl up into his arms all night and let him hold me. I wanted to wake up with my head on his chest and a warm feeling in the pit of my stomach.

But I was supposed to hate him for killing Ben. *Supposed to.*

After Cristian fell asleep last night, I should've left, like I'd promised him I would. Still, I'd found myself lying in bed next to the man I hated and feared the most, staring up at the ceiling fan spinning around and around and around and wondering if I even *wanted* to leave anymore.

Now that I remembered who he was, I loathed the fact that I'd had the biggest crush on him when we were just kids. I had blocked out that entire part of my childhood and believed the lies my parents had spewed to me about my grandfather. I had forgotten everyone who had once meant the world to me.

My mind traveled to Willy—the poor boy we used to hang out with by the river—and I sucked in a breath. Had Cristian really killed him for kissing me during one stupid Truth or Dare game we played? We had just been kids at the time, no older than ten.

Cristian arched a brow from across the table. "What are you thinking about?"

I stabbed a sliced banana with my fork and glared at him. "Nothing."

The waiter glanced over at the table again, and Cristian excused himself. I watched him clutch on to the man's shoulder and whisper something into his ear, then disappear into one of the back hallways. I slumped down in my seat and pulled out my phone, glancing at Willy's contact.

I dialed his number.

"The number you have dialed is not in service."

When I tried to text him, the message didn't even send. Though I didn't want to think about my past anymore, I scrolled through my Contacts to find that one boy I had gone on a date with during my first year of college, the guy I'd had to push off me after he put his hand down my pants.

I called him.

"The number you have dialed is not in service."

I swallowed hard and glanced at Cristian, who sat back down across from me, pulling down the cuffs to his white button-up shirt.

A new waitress came over and grinned at us. "How are we doing over here?"

"We're good," I said, wanting her to just leave already. So many questions were rushing through my mind. When she finally left, I leaned across the table and bit my lip. "Did you really kill Willy?"

Cristian stuck a forkful of eggs in his mouth like it was nothing. "Yes."

"I don't believe you," I whispered.

Truth was, I *did* believe him. I just didn't *want* to believe him.

Cristian scrolled through the photos on his phone, tapped on a video, and handed his phone to me. I took it in my shaky hands and gazed emptily as Willy stared up at the camera with bruised red eyes and chains wrapped around his ankles, attached to cinder blocks. One of the blocks was pushed off the side of a dock and into the river. Willy's body followed.

My eyes widened slightly, and I pushed the phone back to him. "Why?"

"Because you're mine, *principessa*. I can't leave anyone alive who's ever touched you the way I will…"

"So, does that mean you'll kill your men too?"

"My men say as I say, touch as I say, do as I say. Willy didn't. He touched you without permission. Your permission or *mine*. I'd never be able to accept the way you two were together. With my men, it was my order to ruin your pretty little face …"

He leaned across the table and brushed his thumb against my lip. I smacked it away.

His lips curled into a cruel smirk as he sat back. "But perhaps, one day, I will kill them for you."

"You are fucking crazy," I whispered. "Why do you have that video?"

He deleted the video. "Because I knew you'd ask once I told you."

My eyes widened, and I shook my head at him. "And what happened to our waiter?"

Cristian clenched his jaw and sat back. "Eat your food. We're leaving soon."

27

cristian

"I THOUGHT you said we were leaving?" Roxie asked me with her arms crossed over her chest, making her breasts look bigger. "For the millionth time today, I just want to go home to cry." She tilted her head and sneered at me, "And get the hell away from you, you psychopath."

I tore my gaze away from her breasts, trying hard to forget spending last night with her. I'd promised myself that I wouldn't touch her until she proved herself to me. I fucking swore that I wouldn't. But I had broken that damn vow and didn't regret it.

"Tonight."

"Tonight?!" Roxie said, throwing her hands in the air. "Why? I don't want to spend another moment with you."

I tightened my hand on the steering wheel and clenched my jaw to keep my cool. She had a fucking way of crawling under my skin and staying there. I fucking hated it sometimes. Nobody made me feel so infuriated.

After parking the car in front of a gun range, I reached into the backseat and pulled out a box with the gun that Chiara had selected for Roxie. She had even etched her initials in the grip, like her father had done with hers. Though Chiara wasn't my family, she was a close ally that could do Roxie some good.

I set the box on Roxie's lap and nudged her. "Open it."

She scrunched her nose at it and hesitantly opened the box. "Wow, what a great present to try to impress me …" Roxie shoved the box back into my hands. "I don't want your stupid gun. I already told you that I'm not killing anyone."

Once I pulled her out of the car, I grabbed the gun in one hand and Roxie's in the other, tugging her toward the entrance of the shop. "You need to learn how to use one for protection," I said to her. "There are a lot of people who will want to kill you, including that woman you met the other night. If you don't know how to use a gun, then you'll die."

Roxie rolled her eyes, as if she was annoyed, but didn't put up a fight as we walked into the shop.

I nodded to one of my many cousins, stopped at the range, and put the gun in Roxie's hand. "Shoot it."

After glaring at me, Roxie aimed toward the target at the very end of the range and shot the gun, the kickback making her stumble. The bullet went into another person's target. She glanced at our target and frowned.

"You know, I'm only doing this to be able to kill you one day," she said, aiming again.

I placed my hands on her shoulders and pushed them down slightly, so she would relax. "If you could actually aim, maybe, one day, you will," I said, leaning closer to her and steadying her hips. "Now, look down the sight, aim for the middle circle, and follow through with it."

Though Roxie tensed with me behind her, she looked down the sight and pulled the trigger. The bullet whizzed through the air and shot right through the very edge of our target. It was something, but not good enough.

We stayed at the shooting range for two hours, perfecting Roxie's aim. She had hit about everywhere, except the center of the target, and was getting frustrated with it. Yet, instead of giving up, she continued to mutter how she was learning this to kill me one day and promised me that she would.

"Let's take a break. You'll never hit it when you're angry."

"You can shoot someone when you're angry," she said back. "I can too."

She aimed one more time, pulled the trigger, and watched the bullet pierce through the corner of the target. She shook her head and reloaded her gun. "This is so damn stupid. I don't even want to"—she pulled the trigger—"do"—she pulled the trigger again—"this."

When she finished, I took the gun out of her hands and tried to keep my cool. "We'll work on it later. For now, you'll stay with me, so I know you're safe."

"I already told you that I don't need your protection."

"Why can't you just accept my fucking help?" I asked, snapping.

Why did she have to try hard to get on my nerves every chance she got? She couldn't come easily or quietly, had to make a huge deal out of the smallest gestures.

Roxie threw her tattooed arms into the air, brown eyes widening. "Because you kill people! You sell drugs! You do illegal shit and hurt people for your own benefit! Why the hell do you think I don't want your help? I don't want to go to jail for *your* fucking mistakes. If you—"

Before she could speak another word, I slapped a hand over her mouth and pushed her into another room. Struggling against me, she smashed her hands against my chest and tried hard to get out of my hold. But I didn't let her go until the door was secured shut.

"You can't fucking scream that shit to all of Boston," I sneered at her.

Nobody else had dared to fucking talk back to me, never mind tried to get me fucking arrested, like she just had. She said what was on her mind and didn't give a fuck about who heard it.

"If any one of my men did that, they'd be fucking dead by now."

"Well, it's good that I'm not one of your men, huh?"

"You know, Roxie, for a split fucking second, I was going to let you off the hook and give you a fucking pass to not kill that man, but screw that. If you don't want my help or my protection, bring me that man's head, and I'll stop."

It was a lie. She and I both knew it. I would never let her leave me, never stop protecting her.

But she wouldn't be able to do it, not now anyway. I knew it, and I was banking on this making her stick around because I knew if I forced myself upon her, we'd be fucking married tomorrow, and she would loathe me for everything that I was.

"You said that last time." Roxie stepped back and crossed her arms. "And you still fucked me, like I wanted you to."

Brat. She was a fucking brat.

"Well, I fucking mean it this time."

Roxie uncrossed her arms and smirked at me, as if she had one-upped me. "There are other ways to get you to touch me like that again. I assure you, Cristian, you don't have more control of me than I have of you."

I grasped her by the neck. "Like you flirting with Marco?" I asked, keeping my gaze focused on her so I wouldn't fucking break something. At the fucking sight of him touching her the other night, I'd almost lost it. "You flirt with him again, and I'll make you put a bullet straight through his head."

She didn't back down because she didn't think I'd actually do it. He was the best fucking man I had in this family, most loyal too … except when it came to Roxie. And I fucking hated the bastard for that. I didn't know how many times I had to prove to her that I'd do anything to have her as my wife, but I'd do it over and over and over until it was burned into that pretty mind of hers.

28

roxie

THOUGH CRISTIAN HAD KILLED man after man in front of me, I didn't think he'd actually kill Marco. He had trusted Marco enough to watch me overnight, hadn't killed him already for merely helping me, and had put his trust in Marco probably since he had taken over this business.

Killing him would be more of a hassle. It'd probably be easier for him to just let me go, like he should've done a long time ago.

"Do you understand me?" Cristian asked, cold and devilish eyes fixed on me. He strummed his fingers down the column of my neck. "Hmm?"

The way he talked to me, the way he had taken me, the damn way he had already touched every part of my body … I hadn't been able to get it off my mind all night. And him standing this close to me wasn't helping.

I swallowed hard and pressed my knees together, feeling the heat gather in my core.

"Do. You. Under—"

I laughed at him—full-on laughed in his face. It must've been his craziness rubbing off on me, or I had a death wish. Probably the latter.

"Listen, Cristian," I said, wrapping a hand around his wrist. With my other, I placed it right on the front of his pants, feeling his already-hard cock. "The only thing I understand is this."

Cristian closed his eyes and mumbled something in Italian under his breath, the words coming out low and raspy, making my heart race just a bit faster.

Instead of pulling my hand away—like I should have if I hated him as much as I told myself I did—I stroked his cock through his tightening suit pants and imagined him shoving it inside of me again, the thick shaft stretching me out.

Before I could stop myself, I slipped my hand into his pants and wrapped my fingers around his hard, bare cock. I closed my eyes and blew out a deep and unsteady breath.

"Fuck," I whispered, clenching.

Suddenly, Cristian pulled my hand from his pants, twirled me around, shoved my chest against the door, and held me there with his forearm pressed hard against the back of my neck. "What don't you understand about behaving?" he sneered in my ear, voice low and husky. Though I expected him to pull himself away, he fumbled with his pants, pulled out his huge cock, and ground himself against my ass through my thin dress.

"You're the one who"—Cristian pulled up the back of my dress, forcefully pulled my hips toward him, swiped my underwear to the side, and pressed his cock against my aching hole—"doesn't know how to"—he shoved himself inside of me in one quick thrust—"behave."

Overcome by a wave of pleasure, I grasped on to a shelf near the door to hold myself up and moaned out as Cristian pounded himself into me so savagely, just like he had last night. My eyes fluttered closed, and I silently thanked Cristian for shutting the door earlier.

Balls slapping against my clit with every thrust, Cristian curled his finger around my hips every time my pussy tightened harder around him. "Fucking ride my dick, Roxie," he ordered, slowing his thrusts.

I moved my hips back and forth on his, letting him get deep inside of me.

"That's my good *principessa*." Cristian grunted behind me, his voice becoming raspier by the second. "Keep moving your hips like that for me and come on this dick."

As soon as the words left his mouth, I clutched on to the shelf and stopped as wave after wave of pleasure shot through me. I slapped a hand over my mouth and screamed into it. Cristian grunted behind me and stilled too, his cum spilling into me.

"Never having sex with me again, huh?" I asked, mocking him after he pulled out.

All the light, happy pleasure drained from his face. He clenched his jaw, dressed, and grabbed me by the wrist, yanking me out of the room. "This stays in Boston, Roxie. We're leaving."

29

roxie

CRISTIAN HADN'T SPOKEN to me in three days straight. After we returned from Boston, he either stayed at his office or in his penthouse, only making eye contact with me at the club a few times. I knew that he had been watching me though—could feel his eyes on me every time I had my head turned.

I yawned and sat up in my bed, quickly adjusting to my new life as an innocent woman, using the Ricci family's money because the don wanted me for some ungodly reason.

After eyeing the gun Cristian had given me—which I hadn't touched since Boston—I decided that I'd find a shooting range around here and try it out again. If I was going to kill him one of these days, my skills needed to be perfect. Absolutely perfect.

Wearily, I dressed, grabbed the gun, and tucked it into my waistband. Someone knocked on my door, and I hurried to it, hoping it was Cristian. When I opened the door, Cristian wasn't there, but the new guard he had assigned to me was.

"What?" I asked, brow arched.

After walking out of the apartment and locking the door behind me, I hurried to the elevators, not waiting for the guard to even follow. I jammed the bottom floor button until the doors started to close. The guard stepped into the elevator just before the doors closed.

"You slept late. I just wanted to make sure you were okay."

"Where is the closest shooting range?" I asked.

"Two blocks down, a few buildings away from Cristian's club."

After deciding to walk, I found myself standing at the doors to an upscale, exclusive shooting range. I hadn't even thought that there'd be one this close, never mind this central in the city. I walked down three sets of stairs, down into a deep underground basement, and gave the pretty brunette at the counter the best smile that I could muster.

"I'm sorry," she said, flashing me teeth so white that I thought I had gone blind for a moment. "This area is restricted. You need a platinum membership to use our facility. And it looks like platinum is just a smidgen out of your price range."

"Excuse me?" someone said from behind me. Chiara appeared at my side, giving the woman a glare hard enough to kill. "Do you know who you're speaking to?"

All the blood drained from the woman's face. "Ms.—"

"Cristian Ricci's girlfriend," Chiara continued, placing one hand on her hip.

I nearly cringed at the label but held myself together because I wanted to get in and practice.

"If he found out that you weren't allowing his precious girl-friend into your facility, do you know what he'd do to you?"

"I'm so, so sorry. Please ..." She stood and opened the door for us. "Please, head into the range."

After the woman shut the door behind us, Chiara looped her arm around mine and led us to a range. Some men looked over and nodded to her, showing her respect.

"So, I see that Cristian gave you the gun," she said, tugging it right out of my waistband. She cracked a smile. "You're going to have to hide it better than that if you want to blend in with the family."

I smoothed out my shirt and took my gun from her, lining up at the range. "I don't plan on blending in."

"That's what I told Cristian before you left for Boston," she said.

After taking my first shot and hitting the edge of the target, I glanced over at Chiara, who shot five bullets right in the center of hers.

"He seems to think you can be tamed. You can let him think that, but … we both know who really runs the relationship."

"Cristian and I are not in a relationship," I clarified. "I hate him."

After a few moments, she looked over at me. "Hate? Is that why you were shooting Alessa death glares the other night when she was telling you to stay away from Cristian?"

"Alessa?" I asked, her name tasting so sour on my tongue. I aimed at the target and blew out a deep breath.

"Alessa, the Ricci family whore. She and Cristian used to date a couple years or so ago."

"They what?"

"Used to date," Chiara said.

I shot the gun, and the bullet pierced the dead center of the target. Whoever this Alessa girl was … I needed to have a little chat with her.

30

roxie

FOR THE NEXT THREE HOURS, Chiara stayed with me at the gun range, chatting about everything from Cristian to Alessa to all the other girls that I had to worry about now. I shouldn't have gotten so angry. I didn't like Cristian. I just liked the sex he gave me. That was all.

Definitely.

Yet I couldn't help but feel jealousy and anger pool in the pit of my stomach. I had already hated that woman after she threatened me. But … I hated her even more now.

"Well, I have some business to take care of," Chiara said, walking with me out of the shooting range. "Let's get together later this week. I can bring you shopping. Those clothes that Cristian bought you are definitely not your style. I know a place that is."

After saying goodbye to her, I strutted to the club, needing a drink after everything I learned this week about my past and about Cristian and his. Though it was the middle of the day, the bar was packed with CEOs and businessmen, people who looked too rich for their own good, all drinking and having a grand time.

I decided not to look for Cristian and cozied up to the crook of the bar instead. The bartender placed an Afterglow sangria in front of me, but I pushed it away.

"Sambuca, please."

Marco walked out of that back hallway, one hand stuffed into his pocket. He slid into a chair on the other side of the central bar and swiped his hand across his face, looking tired. When he looked up, he made eye contact with me, his eyes lingering longer than they should've.

I didn't offer him a smile but held eye contact as the bartender handed me a glass and I sipped the drink. From the corner of my eye, I caught Alessa in the hallway with her nasty hands rubbing all over Cristian's chest. Cristian moved closer to her and said something that I couldn't quite understand or read. Yet she smiled even wider.

Overcome with anger, I placed my drink down on the bar, sauntered over to Marco, and grabbed him by his hand. "I need to talk to you."

"Roxie, I can't—"

I glared at him. "In the back room. Now."

Screw Cristian's warning about killing Marco. He wasn't going to do it anyway, and I wanted to make him jealous.

31

roxie

THOUGH I TOLD myself that I really wanted to rip off Marco's clothes in the back room and let him fuck all my worries away, I found myself shutting and locking the door and glaring at him. He stuffed his hands into his pockets and leaned against the wall, making sure to keep his distance.

"Who is Alessa?" I asked him, tapping my foot against the wooden floor.

He had been with Cristian for so long that he ought to know more about her than Chiara did.

"I want to know everything you know about her. Don't give me that *I don't know what you're talking about* shit either. I know that she used to date Cristian."

Marco rolled his eyes and sighed a breath of relief. "For fuck's sake, Roxie, if you wanted to know more about her, we could've talked out there." He mumbled something in Italian and made the damn sign of the cross, as if he was thanking whoever looked down upon him for another day of life in this gangster world.

"I'm waiting."

"Let's talk out there, so Cristian doesn't think we're fucking."

When he went to open the door, I stepped in front of it.

"No." I pointed to the couch. "Sit down and tell me everything I need to know. I don't want to wait any longer, and I know you'll try to get out of it as soon as we leave this damn room."

After staring at me for a few moments, Marco sighed again and sat on the couch. "What do you want to know? You already know that they dated. There's not anything else you need to know, except that she's trouble, right?"

"How long?" I asked, hands balling into tight fists. "How long were they together?"

Marco paused and shrugged. "Beats me."

"How. Fucking. Long?"

"Nine months," Marco finally said after a few more moments of silence.

"How does he know her?"

Marco stood back up and waved his hands in the air. "I don't want to get in the middle of this. This is his drama. He's probably looking for me. I have to g—"

I pulled my gun from my purse and stuck it against his rib cage just as he was about to leave the room. He froze for a moment, then relaxed and turned around to face me.

"Someone showed you how to hold a gun," he said. "I'm impressed, but we both know you're not going to actually shoot me."

He was right.

But I wasn't going to back down.

I pushed it harder against his ribs. "Give me fucking something about her."

"Cristian's sister and Alessa are best friends. Alessa has been whoring around with the entire family since Cristian broke it off with her. She wants him for his money. That's all the women around here want from him." Marco blew out a deep breath. "Anything else the queen wants to know?"

After dropping the gun by my side, I frowned. Something about that last part made me sad for Cristian. Even though Cristian could buy anything he ever wanted, he couldn't buy people who actually cared about him. In his kind of business, who could you really trust?

I scrunched my nose. What the hell was I thinking? I didn't care about him.

But he cared about me, right?

"That's all," I said, wanting to just go home and sink into the bedsheets with a bottle of Afterglow to forget about today, yesterday, and all the days before then.

I pulled the door open, tucked the gun back into my purse, and walked out the door with Marco following behind me.

Before he could get lost in the crowd, I grabbed his wrist. "Don't tell Cristian that I asked."

32

cristian

"HOW MANY TIMES do I have to tell you to get your fucking hands off me?" I asked Alessa.

She trailed a finger down my chest and dropped her hand, rolling her big, makeup-dressed eyes at me. "What is your problem? You've been moody for the past few weeks. I just want to have fun, like we used to."

From the corner of my eye, I saw one of the doors in the back hallway open. Roxie walked out of it with Marco trailing behind her. She grabbed his wrist and pulled him closer to her, whispering in his ear. I balled my hands into fists, aching to end that man's life right fucking now.

Was I jealous of him? Fuck yes. I wasn't going to fucking deny it. I had stupidly let him touch what was mine, and now, he thought he could do it all the fucking time. Roxie wasn't any better, using him to get on my fucking nerves.

"I'm talking to you," Alessa said, grabbing my chin and yanking it toward her.

I captured her wrist in my hand and shoved her away. "Next time you touch me, I'll put a bullet straight through your head. I don't give a fuck if you're my sister's best friend. I'll fucking kill you."

Alessa smirked at me. She always fucking loved to drive me crazy in the worst possible ways, which might've been what initially drove me to her. But not now. Now, she was just plain annoying, and I couldn't get my sister to give her up as a friend.

"Oh, Cristian, I love that dirty mouth of yours." She pulled a wad of lipstick from her purse and puckered her lips. "I'll see you later, and … don't forget to tell your little friend *Roxie* that Alessa says hello." She turned on her heel and walked through the crowd of people to the exit.

I followed after her. "Don't touch Roxie. Don't even *think* about touching Roxie."

She smirked at me. "Do you really care about her that much? You used to love me as much as you love her. Do you remember that, Cristian? Remember taking me out to breakfast in Boston, killing any man who looked at me, letting me stay with you?" She bit her lip after speaking lies.

I had never killed anyone for her. I killed one man in front of her because he had betrayed me, not because he had insulted her. But I had killed more people than I would ever admit for Roxie, and I'd do it again and again.

Though I had let Alessa stay with me and I had brought her out to breakfast. This life was fucking lonely sometimes. I didn't know who to trust and who just wanted me for my money. Most of the time, those people were the same. Sometimes, those people were snakes, like Alessa.

"Don't you want someone who will kill with you? Be your partner? Roxie will never do that. She'll never live up to be the woman I could be and have already been for you, Cristian. Remember that."

She walked through the exit doors and out of my damn club.

When she was gone, I grabbed the bouncer's shoulder. "Next time you let her into my club, it'll be your balls. Don't fall for it when she rubs her tits all over you. One more mistake, and she'll be the death of you."

33

roxie

"WHAT THE FUCK were you doing with Marco in *my* back room?" Cristian asked me, grabbing my upper arm and pushing me to a dark corner of his club. "Huh? What did you fucking do with him?"

I balled my hands into fists and ripped myself away from him, feeling the anger pool inside of me. "What were you doing with Alessa? Why were her hands all over you? Why did she walk out of the hallway with you?"

The more questions I asked him, the more I sounded jealous.

Was I really jealous of Alessa? Did I really care about what they did together? Did it really bother me that she and Cristian had slept together countless nights before, touched each other, kissed each other?

Yes. Yes. And yes.

Why?

Because I …

Because I …

I fucking liked him.

Not that much. Barely at all. But I did. Just a bit.

"That's none of your business," Cristian said to me.

"None of my business?!" I shouted louder than I should've. A couple of people looked over at us, but I didn't give a fuck. "If it's none of my business, then what I do with Marco is none of your business."

Cristian clenched his chiseled jaw and stepped away from me, raising his brows as if something finally made sense to him. "You're jealous of her, aren't you?" he asked me, then laughed right in my face. "You're jealous of Alessa?"

"Don't say her fucking name," I snapped.

The corner of Cristian's lips curled up. "All along, I thought you hated me."

I shoved my hands against his chest. "Shut up."

Something must've clicked in Cristian's mind because his facial features seemed to relax even more. "You do know that if I asked Alessa to kill the man that I'd asked you to, she would've pulled the trigger already."

My nostrils flared, and I crossed my arms. "Well then, fucking ask her if you like her so much."

Cristian suddenly got quiet. "I asked you to do it. Not her because I want you to kill without thinking about it. You don't have time to fucking think when you're getting shot at. All I asked was that you kill one person to prove yourself to me, one man who had done the same thing to some child that your grandfather had done to you."

"And I told you that I didn't want to kill anyone," I said through clenched teeth.

Knowing that the man he had asked me to kill had molested a child did change my mindset a bit for me, but ... I didn't want to kill *anyone ever*. I couldn't imagine ending someone's life just by pulling a trigger. Just the thought was traumatizing.

"Fuck!" Cristian threw his hands up in the air and turned around, the gun stuck in his waistband on full display for me.

It was dark in here, but I could see the light's reflection off the side of it.

When he turned back to me, his whole relatively calm demeanor that he usually had with me had vanished and was replaced with that sinister look he had given Charlie right before he hammered that nail into his skull. "I fucking have to teach you this the hard way, don't I?"

He went to grab my arm, but I yanked it away.

"Don't touch—"

He reached for my arm again and captured it, shoving me onto my knees in the corner of the club. After pulling the gun from the back of his waistband, he pressed it against my head. All my feistiness and brattiness disappeared almost immediately.

Though I knew he wouldn't pull the trigger, what if his finger slipped?

"This is what it feels like to stare death right in its face," Cristian said, shoving the muzzle harder against my temple, the cool metal making me shiver. "One moment, you're alive, and then the next, you're fucking dead, Roxie. One moment, you're having lunch on a yacht, and the next, you're drowning in a sea of your own blood. You don't want that."

"Says you," I spat up at him.

He chuckled lifelessly, pulled the gun away from my temple, and stuck the muzzle right between my lips, pushing as much of the barrel into my mouth as he could. "You fucking want this, Roxie? You fucking want me to pull the fucking trigger?"

Mouth stuffed full with his Glock, I froze. Tears welled up in my eyes. I might not know why I'd kept fighting him before, but I knew my reason for fighting him now. I didn't think that I was good enough for him. So many late nights, I'd wondered where Ben was, believing he was cheating on me with someone prettier, and now ... fucking watching Alessa put her filthy hands all over Cristian made me jealous. And we weren't even dating.

Yet, if I was going to kill anyone, it would be her.

"Answer me, Roxie," Cristian said, pulling the gun out of my mouth.

I spat up some spit and looked around the room to see if anyone had been watching. Nobody. Nobody had noticed a damn man putting a gun to my head, except Marco. I wiped the tears from my cheeks. Cristian followed my gaze, saw his right-hand man, and growled.

Fucking growled.

He pushed the muzzle of the gun back into my mouth. "You want to be desperate for fucking attention, Roxie? Show me how fucking desperate you are for Marco's fucking attention." He grasped my chin and forced me to look up at him as he stuck more of the barrel into my mouth.

Looked like I wasn't the only one who was jealous.

He sneered at me, "Suck it."

34

roxie

CRISTIAN STUFFED MORE of the gun into my mouth and draped his other hand around my throat. Like the crazy, fucked up bitch I was, I wrapped my lips around the barrel, sucked my cheeks in, and stared up into his devilish brown eyes.

Bodies were pressed together, scantily clad waitresses strutted around in high-heeled black boots, and men were drunk off their asses. Club lights flashed around us; more people crowded into the room. Yet nobody saw little ol' Roxie in the dark corner, on her knees, sucking off something that could murder her with the pull of a trigger.

"Suck it," Cristian ordered again, turning the gun sideways.

I placed my hands on his knees and bobbed my head, warmth pooling between my legs. What the fuck was wrong with me? I didn't know, didn't think I'd *ever* know. But I fucking loved every second of this more than I'd ever thought I would.

He took my hand and placed it on his twitching bulge. "You're the only fucking woman who can make me this fucking hard, Roxie." He grasped my chin again and harshly stroked my jaw with his thumb. "The only fucking woman."

My tongue glided across every inch, every crevice of the barrel. I closed my eyes and moved my head faster, pretending that it was Cristian's cock in my mouth, and then I slipped my hand into my pants and touched myself.

It was wrong in every fucking way, but my pussy ached to be filled by him again.

"Fuck me, Cristian," I mumbled on the muzzle, slobber rolling down my chin. I shoved two fingers inside my pussy and whined, the pressure building up inside me already. I bobbed my head some more on the barrel until I made myself gag. "Fuck me, please."

He yanked me to my feet by the arm and pushed through the crowd to his office with his spit-coated gun in his other hand, walking around like he didn't care who saw him. After pushing past some of his guards, he shoved me into the room, slammed the door closed, and thrust me against his desk.

As he savagely undid his pants and pulled out his hard cock, I shimmied out of my pants and spread my legs, showing off my sopping wet pussy. He wrapped his arms around my legs, pulled my ass to the edge so forcefully that my back slammed against his desk, and rammed himself into me.

When I parted my lips to let out a moan, Cristian stuffed the gun back into it. My eyes widened slightly as it hit the back of my throat, and I gagged up spit. I grasped his wrist and stared up at the man who did nothing but scowl.

"I didn't give you permission to stop sucking."

As he continued to pound into me, I sucked weakly on the barrel. He wrapped a hand around my throat and used his grip on me to fuck me faster and harder, to get deeper into my pussy.

"Fuck, *principessa*, you look so sexy like this. Wide brown eyes. Fiery mouth stuffed full with my gun. Rosy-red cheeks sucked in. Brow furrowed the more I fuck you over the edge."

I clenched, heat rushing to my core, and moaned out on the gun. After a few moments, he growled like the monster he was, pulled the gun from my mouth, and pulled me toward him, his fingers strumming against my neck. Forehead resting against mine, he thrust his tongue into my mouth and kissed me hard.

With every passing moment, the pressure rose higher in my core.

"Cristian," I mumbled against his lips, gripping his taut shoulders. "Cristian, I'm going to … I'm going to come." My legs trembled around him.

"Don't fucking come yet," Cristian ordered. He pulled away from me and shouted over his shoulder to the door, "Marco!"

My eyes widened slightly as I clenched harder around him.

A few moments later, someone knocked on the door.

"Yes, boss?" Marco said through the door.

Cristian stared at me like the wild man he was and clenched his jaw. "Come the fuck in my office," he ordered.

The door opened, and Marco walked into the room, staring at us.

Cristian moved his head to the side and scowled. "Roxie"—he slammed hard into me—"is"—he rammed his cock into me again, and my toes curled—"*mine.*"

I threw my head back and came all over his hard cock, screaming out his name, lost in a sea of pleasure. Lips trembling, I grasped his shoulders to hold myself upright as my pussy pulsed around him. "Cr-Cristian."

He grunted and stilled. When he pulled out, his thick cum leaked out of me. He caught some on his fingers and stuffed his fingers into my mouth, watching me suck them off willingly.

"All fucking mine, Marco. Nobody makes my *principessa* feel good, except me. Don't overstep again, or it's your life."

35

cristian

IT WAS GETTING SO FUCKING difficult to ignore Roxie. Ever since I'd tasted her, I had been craving her more than I should. I had waited so many years for her, had gone without her for so long, that I'd stupidly thought I could touch her and hold myself back.

"You understand me?" I asked Marco, stuffing my fingers deeper into Roxie's mouth.

She sucked them so willingly that if I didn't know better, I'd say she was submissive to my touch. But Roxie hated me for everything I was—she reminded me of that every time I saw her.

Marco looked between Roxie and me, then nodded. "Yes, boss."

I waved a dismissive hand. "Go. I don't want to see you."

When he disappeared into the hallway, I looked back at Roxie. Eyes hazy with lust, Roxie continued to suck on my fingers and leaned back against the desk, chest rising and falling quickly.

"Cristian," she murmured, eyes shutting softly. She grabbed for my suit jacket and pulled me toward her. "Cristian ..."

I loved the sound of my name on her swollen purple lips.

"Yes, *principessa*?"

She reopened her eyes and relaxed underneath me. "Take me home."

Roxie wanted me to take her home? Me? She had always angrily stomped out of my club and down the street as I watched from the windows. She never wanted me to bring her home, but I wasn't going to make her ask me twice.

After re-buttoning my pants, I ordered the guard outside my door to start the car. It was a three-block walk back to the building, but I wasn't taking any chances with Alessa being the crazy bitch she was. For all I knew, she was outside the door, waiting for Roxie to leave to kill her. I grabbed Roxie's hand, and she surprisingly let me take it.

"Boss," someone called as I stepped out of the office. "Boss, there's something—"

"Have Marco take care of it," I said, ignoring him and walking to the car through the back door. I opened the passenger door for Roxie, then slid into the driver's seat. "Don't bother me tonight. I'm busy."

Roxie *wanted* me to do something for her *for once*. I wasn't going to let the opportunity pass me by. Maybe I was whipped. Maybe I just wanted her to love me as much as I'd loved her since we had just been children. Maybe I was stupid for it.

She glanced at me from the other side of the car as I drove her home, then looked away. "What happened between us means nothing to me," she said. "I'm not going to be submissive to you, just like all your men are. You don't and will never own me, Cristian."

I clenched the steering wheel hard and pressed my lips together. "You're a terrible liar."

"I'm not lying," she snapped, glaring at me as moonlight glimmered in her eyes.

I pulled into the garage and parked my car, looking over at her.

She flared her nostrils and crossed her arms. "It didn't mean anything. I still hate you."

"If you hated me, you wouldn't have begged me to fuck you."

Roxie exited the car and stormed to the elevators. She stood in the elevator and pressed her floor number. I followed behind her and pressed the top button. When the elevator reached her floor, she went to exit, but I grabbed her wrist and pulled her back in with me.

"You're not staying there anymore."

She struggled against me, fumbling to get out of the elevator, but the doors closed, and we continued up to the top floor.

She yanked herself out of my grip. "I'm not staying with you. I hate you." Fire in her brown eyes, and an angry frown on her lips.

The doors opened, and I gripped her wrist and yanked her out of the elevator with me. "I don't care what you think. You're staying with me tonight, tomorrow, and all the nights after that. You'll be in *my* bed, by my side, sleeping with me. No more getting yourself into trouble."

"I don't get myself into trouble, sleeping alone."

I pushed her into my penthouse and locked the door behind us. She sprinted back to the door, but I grabbed her by the waist and carried her flailing body deeper into the apartment.

"You're not leaving," I said.

She continued to fight against me, but I held her tighter until she stopped.

Part of me thought she just liked to get on my nerves, liked to fight me.

"Are you going to be good if I let you down?"

She grumbled under her breath, and I hesitantly put her down. She glared at me for a few moments, then disappeared somewhere in the apartment. My lips curled into a smirk.

"You're mine, Roxie," I said to myself. "You're never leaving me now."

36

roxie

SOMEONE KNOCKED—MORE like banged—on the door, snapping me out of my deep sleep. I turned and pulled the blankets over my head, hoping the noise would suddenly disappear or that Cristian would get it. My eyes widened slightly at the thought. It sounded like Cristian and I were a thing.

And not like a hookup thing. Like a *thing*, thing.

I didn't even want to officially label us because I didn't even like him *that* much. Just a bit, but not that much to have a long-lasting relationship with him. I gave us a couple of weeks, tops. That. Was. It.

Someone banged on the door again, and I groaned. "Cristian."

No response.

I glanced at the empty bed next to me. That man wouldn't leave me alone last night, had forced me into bed with him all night long. Part of me had despised him for it; the other part of me had loved it.

Lips turning into a frown, I shimmied out of bed, pulled on one of his shirts from his dresser, and searched the house for him. I decided to ignore the front door until I found him. But every room in his penthouse was bare and empty.

"Baby!" a woman shouted from outside the door. "Open up!"

Baby?

Teeth clenched together, I stormed to the door and yanked it open. Dressed in a tight white top, a pink miniskirt, and a necklace that read *Princess*, Alessa stood there with a smirk on her face, as if she had known I'd be here.

"What are you doing here?" she asked.

"What are *you* doing here?" I asked her back, narrowing my eyes.

My fingers curled around the doorframe, and I had the urge to slam the door in her face. But I wanted to know why she was at Cristian's door and calling him *baby*. She couldn't fucking use that name with him. He was mine.

Mine.

"Cristian asked me to come over."

"No, he didn't."

She let out a lifeless laugh and shook her head. "You're clueless. If you knew anything about him, you wouldn't even *think* about sleeping in the same bed as him. He's fucked up, and you can't handle him. You can barely hold a gun straight without cowering in fear. You weren't made for a family like his."

With rage rushing through me, I balled my hands into fists to keep my cool. *My* gun was in the other room. Though I was sure that Cristian had others around the penthouse, I didn't know where the hell he would hide them. I didn't want to turn my back toward her either. God only knew what she would do to me if I did.

"And you were made for this?" I asked, crossing my tattooed arms.

She moved closer to me, her back straight and her eyes narrowed. She thought she was better than me just because she had nicer clothes, more money, and a higher status than me, Ben's stupid, broke ol' girlfriend.

She poked a finger against my chest. "I've been best friends with Cristian's sister for years. Our fathers worked together. I knew him before he ever knew you. And"—she smirked at me and scoffed—

"I'm not afraid to use my gun for protection or to kill someone I don't particularly enjoy dealing with. You're one of those people."

I pierced my own damn skin with my nails in hopes of keeping my mouth closed because once I went off, I wouldn't be able to stop, and I had no fucking way of protecting myself.

Alessa didn't seem like she was all talk. I had a feeling that she followed through with her promises, no matter how sinister and cruel they might be. Part of me thought that she and Cristian were perfect for each other.

But I pushed that thought away as quickly as it'd appeared.

No way would I let her get inside my head. She might've had Cristian last, but I had Cristian now … kinda. Even if our relationship only lasted for a couple of days, a couple of weeks, or a couple of months, he was mine at the moment. And I didn't give anything up that quickly.

When I didn't respond, Alessa flared her nostrils. "Count this as a warning, *principessa*." Alessa moved closer to me, pulled something out of her purse, and pressed the muzzle of her gun against my abdomen. "Leave Cristian the fuck alone, or I'll put a bullet straight through your *stupid*, pretty little head. And then Cristian will be mine."

37

roxie

I HATED THE BITCH. I fucking hated her more than I hated Cristian.

Aiming my gun at her chest, I unloaded every single bullet and watched as it pierced right through her heart. Or at least, that was what I imagined while I practiced at the gun range. I wished, wanted, ached for that flimsy piece of paper to be her.

After reloading, I fired off fifteen more bullets into the target and set my gun down on the counter, hands trembling in rage. It hadn't even been an hour since my *lovely* encounter with the bitch—I couldn't even think her name—and I was still fucking shaken up.

Not because of her threats. Because I wanted to kill her.

Kill her.

Cristian had asked me to kill over and over and over these past few weeks, and I'd declined every fucking time. But when I had seen her standing at his front door, God, had I wanted to put a bullet straight through her stupid fucking brain.

My phone buzzed in my purse, and Cristian's name appeared on the screen.

Cristian: Get back to our fucking home now. Before I find you.

Rolling my eyes, I pushed my phone back into my purse and picked the gun back up, drawing my fingers against my initials in the side. Yes, I had snuck past the guards in the building. Of course I did. I found a way through a side entrance that wasn't covered.

When the bitch had left, I'd needed to blow off some steam.

I didn't want Cristian bothering me about it. Hell, *he* was the one who had left me alone this morning. If he had stayed, she wouldn't have bothered me.

I tightened my hand around the grip until my knuckles turned white. I'd never wanted this life, never desired to hold a gun, but I couldn't help the way my hand slid around the grip, the way my head tilted slightly to stare down the front sight, the way my fingers pulled the trigger again and again and again until there were no more bullets left.

And it was all because that bitch had shown up this morning.

Fuck her and fuck him for not killing her yet.

If he wanted me in his life—if he really fucking wanted me—he would've dropped her the moment he killed Ben and pursued me. I didn't give a fuck what she was to him or his sister or what she had been. She should've been gone, killed, six feet under by now.

Flaring my nostrils, I pointed the gun, without any bullets, at the target and blew out a deep breath. What was wrong with me? I put the gun down for good. What the fuck was wrong with me? I wasn't going to let her get me angry. Cristian was a one-time, maybe two-time fling. I had already vowed to myself that I'd get rid of him after a few months and once his obsession with me died down.

If Alessa wanted me gone, then that was fine by me.

Cristian: Get your fucking ass back to the house.

Cristian: I'm not going to tell you again.

Raising a brow, I typed a message to Chiara, asking her to go out shopping with me and not to tell Cristian about it. If he wanted to be crazy with me, I was going to be a crazy bitch to him too. I smirked at message after message after message he had sent me and opened them up, so he'd *know* that I had seen them.

Cristian: Where the fuck are you?

No reply.

Cristian: How'd you get past my guards?

No reply.

Cristian: If you make me come out to find you, I'll tie you up and make sure you don't ever leave.

My lips curled into a smile as I cleaned up my station and placed my gun back into my purse. I really needed a girls' day with Chiara to relax and not think about *her* anymore. She didn't deserve my anger or my fear.

And before I stuffed my phone back into my purse, I typed back to him, knowing that he was probably staring his phone down like a madman, waiting for my response.

Me: You won't do that.

I shoved my phone into my purse, tossed the strap over my shoulder, and walked out of the shop and into beautiful New York City, alone for the first time in ages. I had been with Ben for so long and wound up in Cristian's arms. It was finally time for me.

"Over here!" Chiara shouted from a black BMW parked at the curb right in front of a Do Not Park sign.

I arched a brow and walked over. I guessed being part of the Mafia let you do whatever the hell you wanted to do.

She leaned over the center console and opened my door from the inside. "Get in, before anyone sees. Cristian has people out looking for you."

After scooting into the passenger seat, I relaxed and laid my head back against the headrest. Pushing some hair out of my face, I glanced over at her and smiled. Truly smiled. Though running away from Cristian for a day probably wasn't the best idea, it sure gave me a rush, just like the thought of killing Alessa did, but in a totally different way.

"Why the hell are you hiding from him?"

"I stayed in his room last night," I admitted, sinking down in the passenger seat so nobody could spot me as we drove through the streets of New York. "He was gone this morning, and Alessa showed up, threatening to kill me."

Chiara slammed on her brakes. "Shut the fuck up. No, she didn't."

I tightened my hand into a fist. "She did."

"And you didn't tell Cristian?!"

"No."

"Why?" she asked, staring at me with confusion. "He'll kill her for it."

"I don't want him to kill her."

"Why not?"

"Because I want to do it."

38

cristian

ROXIE: **You won't do that.**

I stared at the text message sent hours ago and hurled my phone at the wall.

Where the fuck was she? How'd she slip past my guards? And what if someone had stolen her from me? Everyone in the business was slowly starting to figure out that Roxie and I were a couple. At least, that was what I thought we were. She'd be my wife one day. And I'd make sure that one day was soon once I found her.

If someone wanted to reprimand me for something, all they would have to do was take her.

Torture her.

Fucking hurt what was mine.

"Have you found anything?" I shouted at the guards running in and out of my office. "Any-fucking-thing that will lead me to her? Huh?" I grabbed Roxie's own personal guard by his throat and thrust him against the wall. "You were supposed to be guarding the fucking floor to make sure nobody left. How did you fucking let her get past you?"

Without letting him even speak, I slammed him into the wall

again, pushed him away from me, and pointed at the door. "Get out of my fucking office. I don't want to see you. Find Roxie for me or get out of this fucking city by tonight, before I kill you, you incompetent fuck."

When the man scurried out into the hallway, I slammed the door and growled.

Roxie had left me, and I'd fucking let her. All I needed was to take care of business. I had been gone for forty-five fucking minutes, and she had snuck past all the men I had guarding that building.

Snatching my cracked phone from the ground, I dialed Roxie's number and balled my hand into a fist when it went to voice mail. I called her again and again and again. Nothing. I tried texting her next.

Me: Answer. Me.

Was I desperate to find her? Fuck yes.

Did I care that I sounded pitiful? No.

She was mine. I'd already told her that I wouldn't let her leave. She had. And when I found her, I swore to God I'd lock her in the house outside of the city, where I usually did business, and keep her there as mine. She wouldn't leave my side from now on.

The *Delivered* notification on the messages turned to *Read* before three little bubbles popped up on the screen and then disappeared. I waited five minutes for her reply and concluded that it wasn't coming, not unless I continued to be a prick.

Me: ???

Roxie: Where are you?

Me: At the club, trying not to lose my fucking shit because of you.

Roxie: Cool.

I clenched my jaw and growled, staring down at the phone. God, this woman did nothing but aggravate me. She knew I was fucking worried about her and continued to push me. Nobody ever dared to talk back to me or ignore me like she did. I fucking loathed it and loved it at the same time.

Except now, I didn't love it.

I needed to know she was okay.
Me: Where?
Roxie: Having drinks with Marco. ;)
Roxie: Come and find me.

39

roxie

SMIRKING TO MYSELF, I finished typing the text to Cristian and deposited the phone on the counter. Was it wrong to fuck with him? Eh, maybe. Did I think he deserved it? Definitely yes. He'd left me alone this morning, and that bitch had come for me, threatening me. One day, I'd build up the courage to kill her.

I pulled my baseball cap down further to cover my face as I sipped my white sangria in the middle of Cristian's club. It had been surprisingly easy to sneak in here without anyone noticing. Most of his guards and men were gone for the night, doing something, and that something was probably looking for me.

Cristian stormed out of his office, slammed the door behind him, and rushed out into the club, the flaps of his suit jacket flying open. Nostrils flaring, brow furrowed, jaw clenched, Cristian looked furious enough to kill someone.

When he stormed past the other side of the bar without spotting me, I let out a deep breath and slumped my shoulders forward. I didn't know why I had come back. I'd escaped from the Mafia and had a chance to flee the state and country even. But for some ungodly reason, I didn't seem to have it inside of me to leave him for good.

Cristian was annoying as fuck, but I liked it. I liked his crazy.

I just didn't like that Alessa was still in his fucking life.

I wanted him.

I wanted all of him.

And I didn't share.

As he escaped through the door, I took another sip through my straw and pushed my empty drink to the edge of the bar, picking up my phone and smiling at Chiara's message that popped up.

Chiara: I'll drop off your clothes tomorrow. Don't have too much fun messing with him tonight. Make sure he knows that I did NOT encourage you at all. ;)

I tapped on the message to type back when someone grabbed me by the back of the neck and yanked me out of the chair, making me drop the phone onto the marble floor. Fingers digging hard into my neck and throat, Cristian thrust me forward and toward the back hallway.

"I asked you one simple question. One simple fucking question," he sneered.

Struggling in his hold, I pushed against his chest and stumbled over my feet. "Let me go."

"No."

"Let me go!" I pushed and shoved him as he continued to drive me to the back exit. I smacked his chest, the side of his face, anywhere that I could, hoping that he'd release his grasp just slightly. "Let me go. I didn't do anything!"

Forcing me into his office, he slammed the door, shoved me to the back closet, and pulled a thick black rope from it. As if he had done this a million times, he grasped my hands in one of his and tied them together behind my back to restrain me—the same way his men had the night he killed Ben.

"Cristian, stop!"

Restraining me completely with the rope until all I could do was squirm, he picked me up, threw me over his shoulder, and walked to his car. "You're mine, *principessa*. You're not leaving me ever again."

40

roxie

"LET ME GO," I said between clenched teeth, staring out the windshield at the dark skyline.

We had left the city about an hour ago now, I thought, though I hadn't been paying much attention because I had been trying desperately to get out of this damn rope. He'd tied it so snug that I could barely move.

Cristian tightened his grip on the steering wheel and clenched his jaw, continuing on the gloomy road.

I jerked back and forth, pounding my body against the leather passenger seat. "Let me go! I'm not going to run off again."

"Where the fuck did you go?"

"Out."

"I'm not playing these fucking games with you." He turned harshly onto a street that I recognized as that family home he had brought me to that one time he tortured Charlie. "You're not leaving me. I spent years trying to get you back."

A furious and emotional wreck, Cristian slammed on the brakes and parked the car when we reached the house. He walked to my side, pulled me out, and threw me over his shoulder.

I squirmed some more, like a damn worm, trying desperately to get out of his hold. "Cristian!"

"Scream all you want, *principessa*," Cristian said to me, walking into the house and up a set of stairs. "There's nobody around for miles."

"Cristian!" I screamed louder, hoping it'd cause him some hearing loss or something.

Anything.

"Why can't you let me go?"

"Why did you leave?" he asked me.

Knowing that he'd kill that bitch himself if I told him that Alessa had shown up at his doorstep earlier, I pressed my lips closed. Adrenaline pumped through my veins as I thought about firing shot after shot into that stupid skull of hers and killing her. I didn't want him to kill her. I needed to do it.

Not only to show Cristian that I could do it, but to also show myself.

Everything that had happened these past few weeks was out of my control. Call me fucking crazy, but if I killed her, I would be the one in control. I wouldn't feel like Cristian was the one making all this happen. It would give me a sense of fucked up freedom again. But ... maybe some jail time too.

Cristian dropped me onto a bed. I landed with a thump and squirmed around on the California king–size mattress, needing to get out of here as quickly as possible. But before I could get far, he restrained me on the bed, each ankle tied to a bedpost, and grabbed a vibrator from a drawer.

I dug my heels into the mattress to squirm toward the headboard, but didn't make it anywhere. Cristian turned the toy on, crawled between my parted legs, and shoved it inside of me so forcefully that I screamed out.

"If you want me to treat you just like someone else I torture to get information out of, I will."

Arching a brow, I said, "Torture? You think this is torturing me?"

He turned it up at a higher speed. "I don't think it is. I know it is."

Heat gathered between my legs, pressure building in my core. I stared down at him and clenched my jaw, my toes curling as pleasure ran through my body. He seized my nipple between his fingers and tugged on it harshly.

"Stop it!" I said, flaring my nostrils.

For a brief moment, he stopped to increase the vibrator's speed. My body jerked into the air, pleasure and pain shooting through me. He captured my nipples between his fingers again and tugged even harsher this time.

"Why did you leave?" he asked, squeezing harder.

"I fucking hate you."

He increased the intensity. An orgasm ripped through my body, my clit swelling under the vibration. I bit my lip to feel another orgasm starting to build up and up and up inside my core.

He grabbed my throat in his large hand, seething down at me. "Why did you leave?"

"Go to hell, where you belong, Cristian."

Another higher speed.

"God, fuckin—" I bit my lip to hold back a whimper as another orgasm shot through my body. "Fu-fucking hell ..."

How many speeds does this damn thing have? How is it moving so quickly and so intensely?

My sensitive clit ached as the vibrations continued, even after I hit my peak.

"Why did you leave?" Cristian asked again, strumming his fingers against my throat.

I pressed my quivering lips together. At this rate, I'd be hurting bad within the next few orgasms. But I wasn't going to just admit what had happened at his place. No, I was on a fucking mission to kill that bitch, and nobody, not even Cristian, would get in my way.

41

cristian

I PACED in the hallway outside of the bedroom with my arms crossed over my chest, listening to Roxie moan and scream for me. All I wanted was to barge into the room, take that cheap fucking thing out of her, and push my cock into that throbbing hole of hers. But I had more important things to attend to, like finding out why Roxie had left.

She had been left alone before. She didn't go anywhere. She came back with that sassy-as-fuck attitude the next day and cursed me out in my office, like she usually did. She had never ever left. So why now? And why was she keeping it from me? She hadn't even told me it was because of me yet.

Last night, when I'd brought her home, everything had been fine. Roxie was pissed, like usual, but not pissed enough to leave. She could've snuck out during the night, but she stayed until the morning. I had been waiting all night for her to sneak out, but even after she used the bathroom, she had come back to me.

Snatching Roxie's phone from my pocket, I turned it on to see no new messages. At least she hadn't been off with another guy who was now looking for her. But, fuck, where had she gone? It was eating me a-fucking-live.

Unable to take it anymore, I walked into the room and shut the door behind me, staring at her trembling, tattooed body. "Why did you leave?" I asked her yet again for the umpteenth time today. "Why didn't you tell anyone?"

More importantly, why did she come back?

She grasped at the rope. "Please, take it out of me. Please, stop it. My clit is swollen."

I walked over to the bed, grasped the shiny white handle, and cranked it up to another speed. She whimpered, legs trembling and eyes filled with tears. I both loved and hated seeing her like this, but I needed answers, and she needed punishment.

"Where were you?"

"Fuck you," Roxie said, nostrils flaring. "I already said that I was with Marco."

I clenched my jaw. "Why did you leave?"

She tugged harder on the restraints. "Let me go. I won't fucking do it again."

She would.

"Why. Did. You. Leave?" I asked her again.

Squirming, she shook her head and sank into the mattress. I sighed heavily through my nose and stared at her from the foot of the bed, anger and jealousy rushing through me. All my fucking life, I'd wanted her. All my life. She could've gotten away from me today, lost and never to be found.

I wanted to know why she had left, so I could fix the fucking problem for her.

But I couldn't do that if she didn't talk to me.

I turned the vibrator up another speed.

"Fuck!" Roxie screamed. "Fine! I did it because I don't want anyone else to have you!" she shouted, tears streaming down her face and staining her cheeks. She looked between me and the vibrator between her legs. "Please, stop it. It's hurting me."

I swallowed hard, my hand twitching to pull the vibrator out of her pussy so I could fuck her aching little cunt. Instead, I clenched my jaw and stepped forward, becoming that emotionless man that Dad had taught me to be in situations like this. "What does that have to do with anything?"

She widened her brown eyes and shook her head. "Are you serious, Cristian? Are you fucking serious? I just fucking admitted why I did it, and you can't even accept it." She tried pulling her legs together, but the rope held her back.

"What happened?"

"You left me!" she screamed. "You left me in your damn room. I woke up alone. And I didn't know where you were. Is that what you want to hear? You want to hear that I care about you, too, for some stupid fucking reason? Hmm?"

My hands tightened into fists. She just wanted me to let her go. She didn't like me. She didn't care about me. She had told me that she hated me every single day since *before* the Ben incident. She fucking taunted me about her being with Marco all the time.

I didn't believe her words, though I wanted to. I ached for her to love me. It had been my fucking dream for years now.

Crawling onto the bed with her, I turned off the vibrator and slowly pulled it out of her pussy, watching the way her walls clung to it like they had with my cock, tugging and pulling me back into her. She sighed and relaxed against the mattress, eyes shutting softly.

I fucking cursed myself out for *wanting* to believe her words. I didn't, but I wanted to so much that I crawled between her legs and pretended that she cared about me for just a few moments. I closed my eyes and thrust myself into her tight pussy.

She cried out, brows drawn together, full lips parted. "Cristian, wh-what are you—"

"Shut your mouth, Roxie," I snapped at her, not wanting her to ruin the only instance in our entire lives that I knew I could enjoy. All my life had been shit up to this moment, up until I heard those lies that I so wanted to believe escape her lips. "Let me enjoy this."

42

roxie

WHEN CRISTIAN TOLD me to shut my mouth, I tensed and let him do what he wanted to me—*what I had been wanting him to do to me all damn night.* I didn't know what to do or say; my mind was all over the place. After everything he had done and after I'd admitted that I cared about him, he had told me to … to shove it, basically.

He pushed himself into me forcefully one last time, came, undid the ties around my wrists and ankles, and rolled over onto the other side of the bed, his chest on the mattress and his head facing away from me and toward the bedroom window.

"Roxie," he said under his breath, as if he didn't have much in him to say more.

I drew my knees to my chest and turned onto my side to stare at him. Hesitantly, I placed my fingers on his back and trailed them down one of his many scars, frowning. Was he angry with me for admitting the truth? What did he want me to say to him? I'd thought that he wanted me to want him. Wasn't that what this was all about?

"What's wrong?" I asked him, loathing the silent treatment he was giving me. Ben had given it to me all the fucking time when we dated. And it wasn't like Cristian to be this damn quiet about anything. "What are you pissed about this time?"

Cristian growled, snatched himself away from me, and stood, not once showing me his face. "I have business to take care of."

As he walked to the door, I stumbled out of the bed, my pussy still aching. "Where are you going?"

"Downstairs to the cellar."

"You're not going to stay?" I asked, suddenly feeling so … empty.

"Why would I stay?" he snapped, yanking open the bedroom door but not leaving yet.

"Because I …" I swallowed hard, vulnerability eating me alive. "Because I want you to."

Cristian tensed, the muscles in his back flexing. He paused for a long moment as I stood behind him, worried if I'd said the right thing or not. I didn't want him to think that I was desperate for him. But I … I … I wanted him to be mine.

God, I hated even the thought of it.

But … I couldn't deny it. I couldn't keep lying to him and telling him that I hated him.

In the most fucked up way possible, he had grown on me.

"You can drop the act," Cristian growled, storming down the hallway toward the stairs. "I already let you out of your restraints."

Hurrying after him, I grabbed his hand, forced him to turn around, and pressed my lips to his. Under my touch, he relaxed, his shoulders slumping forward and his hands sliding around my waist. I wrapped my arms around his shoulders and pulled him closer to me, pressing my breasts against his chest and slipping my tongue into his mouth.

After a few moments, I pulled away from him and rested my head against his, staring down between us. I placed my hands on his chest and trailed my fingers down to his hands, wanting to grasp them, but not having enough courage to do so. Instead, I let them drop down by my sides and pulled away from him.

I gave him a half-smile, the best I could muster at least, and turned back around, feeling rejected. I didn't know what it was, if it was me, or why I was even feeling this way. He had kissed me back, but … God, I didn't know. I needed to go to a therapist or something to figure out what had been wrong with me lately.

I had been nothing but an emotional wreck after meeting Cristian.

Before I could make it a mere step, Cristian grabbed my hand and pulled me back. "You're not lying?" he asked, searching my face for any sort of signal that would set him off. Then, he shook his head, as if he had the answer himself. "You're not lying."

"No," I whispered.

"I don't want to believe it," he said quietly, swallowing. He glanced down at his fingers against my wrist and trailed his index finger down the back of my hand and ring finger. "Nobody has ever cared about me. About my money, yeah … but never about me. Never."

"You're not the only one," I said, unsure of what else to say.

I hated feelings. I hated having them, feeling them, thinking about them, *talking* about them. I shrugged my shoulders and looked down at my feet. My parents had basically let my grandfather do whatever the fuck he wanted with me. Ben had used me for years and lied to me over and over again.

Ever since Cristian had started fawning over me … I didn't know how to react or what to even do with him. I hid everything behind a wall, made sure that he didn't know how I truly felt about him. I didn't want to be abandoned or lied to again.

But instead of pushing him away and distancing myself from these feelings, I grabbed his hand and squeezed it tight. "Please, don't go …" I whispered, leaving myself vulnerable. "Don't leave me now. You spent half the night torturing me." I parted my lips to say more, then pressed them closed. This was hard—so damn hard —to say what I wanted to say and not what would make me comfortable. "I want to spend time with you."

43

cristian

"PLEASE, DON'T GO," Roxie whispered again, her cheeks a rosy red and her brown eyes wide in what looked like fear and … vulnerability. She clutched my hand, intertwining my fingers with hers, and held on tight. "I want you."

Unable to hold myself back, I pulled my hand out of hers and grasped her face, kissing her on those plump pink lips and pushing her against the bedroom door. When she inhaled sharply in surprise, I slipped my tongue into her mouth, needing to taste even more of her. I wanted her sweet flavor burned into my memory forever.

I had waited fucking years for this.

Years.

She wrapped her arms around my shoulders, tugged at the ends of my black hair, then sucked my bottom lip into her mouth. After she pulled back, she stared up at me with wide, excited eyes and a cute, lopsided grin, wiping her mouth with her fingers.

Wrapping my hand around her chin, I pushed her back into the bedroom and kicked the door closed with my foot. "Don't fucking wipe my kiss off those lips," I mumbled against her, pressing another sloppy kiss right on her mouth. I brushed my thumb across her bottom lip roughly. "They're mine now."

Roxie giggled. She actually fucking giggled in front of me. *Because of me.* It was a sound I hadn't really heard for years now, and it brought me back to when we had still been young kids, not knowing what the hell was going on but living our lives carefree anyway.

I scooped her up into my arms and dropped her on the bed, lying down beside her and trailing my fingers down her bare abdomen, touching her body, which was really mine for the first time. I had said it over and over again that Roxie would be mine—and not by force either—and now, she was.

It was surreal, and that was saying something because I wasn't an emotional mess, like some of these men out here. Dad had taught me to be coldhearted, to detach emotions from business. But with Roxie, I couldn't. I had never been able to.

"I'm hosting a yacht party tonight," I said, staring into those brown eyes. "I want to show you off, make sure everyone knows you're mine."

"A yacht?" she asked, brow furrowed and eyes wide. "You have a *yacht*?"

"Yes, and you're going to attend the party tonight."

She shot up in the bed and pulled the blankets over her chest, searching around the room, as if she was thinking, then turned back to me. "I can't. I don't have anything to wear. I don't think you'd—"

"You're going." I rolled out of bed, tugged a shirt out of one of the drawers, and pulled it over my head. "I'll arrange for clothes to be brought to you by tonight. I have Charlie downstairs to attend to for now." I tossed her one of the many oversize T-shirts and watched as she shimmied it over herself, her tits swaying as she tugged it over her body, nipples pressing against the fabric. "Come with me."

She stood and smoothed out the shirt. "Actually, I'm going to go with Chiara today. I'm not going to watch you torture that man anymore. You should just k—" She widened her eyes, then pressed her indigo-stained lips together. "I'm going with Chiara. She has my clothes anyway."

I tilted my head, jaw jutting out. "You had me a fucking wreck, and you were just out with Chiara, buying clothes?" I asked through clenched teeth.

She gave me a sinister little smile and shrugged. "Not my fault you don't know how to keep tabs on me. Sorry, not sorry, Cristian. You're going to have to do better than that."

Wrapping my hand around her hair, I grabbed her and tugged her back to me. "Don't think that you got off that easily, Roxie. I still plan to make you the Ricci family's cruelest, most heartless killer." I ran my nose up the side of her neck. "You're never getting out of that one."

44

roxie

"BABE," Alessandro, Chiara's boyfriend—maybe fiancé—called through the high-rise apartment. He stuck his head into the bedroom, holding up his phone, as if to signal *work*, and nodded to me. "See you sometime, Roxie."

After he departed, I followed Chiara into her walk-in closet.

"What do you even wear to a yacht party?" I asked Chiara, flinging through her clothes.

I had actually been surprised that Cristian let me go out with Chiara today while he worked. I hadn't thought he'd let me out of his sight all day after what happened last night.

Chiara grabbed a couple of bikinis from a dresser and tossed one to me. "This."

"I'm not going to fit in this," I said to Chiara, hanging her white string bikini by my finger and narrowing my eyes at her. "If you couldn't tell, my tits are bigger than yours. These little straps aren't going to cover anything."

Chiara grabbed the bikini from me. "Oh, sorry, wrong one. You're not wearing that." She placed another *smaller* bikini in my hand and smirked. "You're going to wear this one underneath your clothes."

"This one is even smaller!"

"That's the point," she said, tugging at my shirt until she successfully pulled it over my head. Then, she eyed my bra and playfully sighed. "You don't know how much I'd pay to have tits like yours. Your body is perfect. No wonder Cristian lusts over you."

I arched a brow and stared into the mirror at my love handles. "My body is not perfect."

"Girl, I try so hard to gain weight." She pulled her shirt off and stared at herself in the mirror, frowning at her thin stomach. "I'd kill for a body like yours." After another moment, she shook her head and turned back to me. "Anyway, back to getting this cute little number on you for Cristian." She returned to pulling at my bra straps until she pulled my bra off.

I covered my breasts with my hands, feeling so exposed. I shouldn't, as most of Cristian's men had already seen me naked before, but Chiara hadn't yet. And being naked was damn vulnerable sometimes.

"How is there a point to wearing this … this *thing*?" I asked as she tied the bikini around my torso.

"You want to make Alessa jealous?" Chiara asked, fumbling with the tie. "Cristian's sister will probably be there tonight, which means that she'll bring along her little minion, Alessa. You wearing this will make that stupid bitch hate you."

"She already hates me."

"Yeah, well, she'll hate you even more, especially when she sees you all over Cristian. Claim your man tonight and make sure she knows not to mess with you because you'll fuck her up. And most of all, don't let whatever she says or does get to you. She wants you to be jealous and react to her. She's a psychopath, just like Cristian."

"You can say that again," I said under my breath, adjusting the bikini in the mirror. My tits basically hung out of it, the tiny pieces of material leaving barely anything to the imagination.

"Also, I might have suggested this, so you can get Cristian jealous. I've seen the way Marco, his second, looks at you. He wants you more than he lets on. Isn't seeing Cristian be a jealous psycho fun too?"

Marco didn't like me at all. He was just … there to blame when I wanted Cristian angry.

I arched a brow in the mirror and turned on my heel toward her, hands on my hips. "I'm beginning to think *you're* the psychopath."

She pulled my hair behind my shoulders and smiled at me. "You're going to learn fast that, sometimes, in a Mafia family, being a psycho is the only way to keep the eyes on you and the slutty hands off your man."

45

roxie

"CHIARA," I whispered, inching closer to her as we walked onto Cristian's yacht. To say that I felt out of place was a damn understatement. I didn't party with the rich, and I certainly never partied with criminals either.

My nerves were getting the best of me, and I wanted to run right off the boat and puke into the ocean beside us. That would surely be a better night than having to play dress-up with a bunch of Mafia men and acting like I had balls as big as them.

I didn't. I just tried to act like it sometimes to protect myself.

"You'll be fine, Roxie. Just take deep breaths."

"Chiara," a young woman with dark brown hair and even darker eyes said to our left, Alessa glaring at me from her side. "I didn't think you'd be here tonight. I thought you'd be out with your boyfriend, like you usually are."

Chiara tightened her grip on my hand, nails digging into my skin. "You mean, Alessandro?" she asked, edginess in her voice and lips curling into an ugly and tense smile. "He's doing just fine. Thanks for asking. He's overseeing some *business* tonight and said that he's *not* sorry for not being able to see your lovely face again."

The woman pressed her full pink lips together and swallowed hard, as if trying to hold back and not start a fight, but I could see it in her eyes that she wanted to rip Chiara to pieces for some ungodly reason. Feeling uncomfortable, I squeezed Chiara's hand harder. I had never gotten dressed up this nice or this slutty, had never gotten into a passive-aggressive fight with someone who could kill me in a moment, and had never been in the presence of someone who actually wanted my head.

"Where's Cristian?" I asked, hoping to ease the tension.

The woman turned to me, one dark brow raised. "Who are you?"

Alessa smirked at me and grabbed my forearm, her nails digging hard into my skin. "Aida, this is Roxie, the whore who keeps hanging around your brother that I have been telling you about." She frowned at me with big, anything-but-innocent eyes. "Didn't I tell you that trash like you doesn't stay around for long?"

Chiara ripped me out of Alessa's grip and stepped closer to her. "Watch your mouth. You're not the only one who plays with guns, Alessa."

And with that, she pulled me away from Cristian's *lovely* sister and the bitch that I'd kill one day. *One day.*

Cristian sat on a couch toward the rear of the yacht, a glass in his hand and a bunch of his men and people I didn't recognize around him. When he spotted me from across the boat, he arched a brow and glanced down at the relatively conservative shirt and skirt that Chiara had made me wear over the bikini.

When she had forced me to put it on earlier, she'd said it was to surprise Cristian with what was underneath.

Though I didn't want to interrupt him and his business—I hated all the business he did—Chiara marched right up to him and pushed me toward him and basically into his lap.

"I'll be back. I have to take care of some things," she said, glaring behind her, as Alessa and Aida walked onto the rear of the boat.

When she disappeared, Cristian wrapped his arm around my waist and kissed me right on the mouth in front of everyone, even Marco, who stood off to the side and watched. While I didn't particularly like the attention from everyone else, having Marco watch us was kind of … fun.

It shouldn't have been, but I had never really gotten much attention from any other man than Ben for the past few years. Even though I'd never do anything with Marco, it was nice to hear that even Chiara thought that Marco had a thing for me. It made me feel wanted and appreciated for once. Either way, I was glad he had come tonight. I needed to speak with him.

"Have you met my sister?" Cristian asked me, nodding to Aida.

I drew my tongue across my teeth and flared my nostrils. "Yes, *Alessa* introduced us."

Cristian tensed underneath me at the mention of her name. "She did?"

"Yes," I said sharply, the tension evident in my voice.

And, almost as if she had heard me, Alessa walked over to us and smiled *sweetly* at Cristian, brushing her fingers against his shoulder. "Cristian, do you have a moment to talk?" she asked him, batting her stupidly fake lashes.

I balled my hands into tight fists, wanting to pound them into her fucking bitchy face.

"I'm busy," he said, digging his fingers into my side.

She leaned even closer to us. "But it's important."

"Alessa," Cristian scolded, cutting his eyes to her, "I'm busy."

"But—"

"Why don't you two chat?" I stood up, arched a brow, and tugged off my shirt in front of everyone, wanting Cristian's attention on me, no matter who tried to chat with him tonight. "I'm going to take a dip in the pool upstairs. Chiara said that you had one."

Cristian grabbed my hand, glared down at my scantily covered chest, and yanked me back to him. "What the fuck are you wearing?"

I shimmied out of my skirt to stand in nothing but the tiny little string bikini wrapped around my body. Everyone stared at me, including Marco, and I smiled back at Cristian innocently.

"Just a bikini," I said, batting my lashes, just as Alessa had. I leaned in closer, as if I were going to kiss him. "I'll see you later." Then, I pulled away from him and strutted past Marco.

"Roxie!" Cristian shouted from the rear of the boat, but I didn't look back.

Alessa could try to tear Cristian away from me, but that possessive man wouldn't be able to think, knowing that I was wearing a bikini two sizes too small around all of his men. Cristian was mine, no matter what she tried to do and no matter how jealous she tried to make me.

All fucking mine.

46

cristian

DRESSED like one of the family sluts, half-naked in a thong bikini and an even smaller top, Roxie walked away from me, swaying her hips from side to side and commanding the attention from even my most loyal men. I balled my hands into fists as Alessa claimed her spot beside me, and I called for Roxie to get back here. I didn't want her walking around the yacht like that.

Before I could stop her, she smirked back at me and disappeared into a hallway that led to the upper-deck pool.

Alessa wrapped her arms around mine, her nails digging into my bicep. "I need to talk to you about some things," she purred. "They're important."

"Get your fucking hands off me," I said through clenched teeth.

She pulled her arms away, crossing her legs and leaning against me with her tits pressed against my arm instead. I clenched my jaw and glared down at her, watching my sister walk toward me from the corner of my eye.

"If you weren't Aida's best friend, I would've killed you by now."

"But you won't," she said with a smirk, tongue sneaking out like a fucking snake. "You already took your father away from her. You don't have the balls to kill her best friend too. You know she'd hate you for that. Now, I want to talk."

Not wanting her to tell my business to everyone, I grasped her by the elbow and pulled her up the stairs onto the upper deck, where I could both keep an eye on Roxie at the pool and talk to Alessa in private. Because that bitch would tell my business to everyone if she got the chance.

"Let's get one thing straight," I said to Alessa. "I didn't kill my parents."

Alessa crossed her arms. "Oh, no? You didn't? Well, Aida thinks you did."

"Because you fed that fucking lie to her," I said through gritted teeth.

"I told her nothing but the truth." She smiled. "Anyway, when are you going to drop the whore? She doesn't get along with anyone in the family and has all your men all over her all the time, especially Marco. It's about time you marry a woman who will kill for you, like you've always wanted."

I flared my nostrils. "That woman was never you."

She drew her manicured fingers up my abdomen. "Believe what you want, Cristian. But when Roxie breaks your heart and cheats on you with one of your men, like your mom cheated on your father … you'll be running back to me."

Glancing over at Roxie, I caught her glaring hard at Alessa, brown eyes blazing with fury, hands balled into fists, jaw clenched hard. I moved closer to Alessa, wanting to see how Roxie would react to me and her, only to see her get even angrier.

I might've been going about this the wrong way for far too long. I didn't need Roxie to watch me kill and torture man after man after man. All I needed was to bring Alessa a bit closer, get Roxie jealous, and make Roxie kill Alessa herself. Then, she'd be what I had set out to make her for years—Manhattan's most heartless killer.

And when Alessa was dead and Roxie needed me to hide the

pathetic, whorish body for her, she'd be forever indebted to me—a debt that could only be forgiven through marriage.

But I wouldn't go out of my way to be with Alessa. Roxie and I were in a good place, and I wasn't going to willingly ruin it in hopes of making her mine for the rest of our lives. But … she couldn't be soft Roxie forever, especially not in this family.

Sooner or later, Roxie would kill, whether it was out of jealousy or self-defense.

47

roxie

CHIARA SWAM UP behind me and poked me in the side. "Girl, *everyone* is talking about you. The girls are jealous. Cristian's men haven't been able to look away." She wrapped her arm around mine and beamed at me. "Our plan is working!"

I arched a brow at her. "Our plan?"

Eyes gleaming underneath the moonlight, she smirked. "Yes, our plan."

Walking to the pool stairs, I glanced over at her. "It was *your* plan, but it's oddly working, though I don't love how many people keep looking over at me. It's kinda weird, especially the older men."

Chiara rolled her eyes and pushed me playfully. "Psh, you love the attention. Any girl would, especially when all eyes are on you and none are on the usual whores who sneak their way into the parties." Chiara moved closer, the water rippling against her. "Imagine how fucking psychotic Cristian would get if your swimsuit accidentally came off in the water."

A laugh escaped my lips, and I splashed her. "That is where I draw the line. Nobody is seeing my tits again unless it's Cristian."

Looping her arm around mine once more, Chiara led me up the stairs and out of the pool, the water rolling down our bodies. She handed me a towel as some of Cristian's men glanced over at us—or more specifically, *me*. "And maybe Marco," she said with a wink.

I glanced over my shoulder and toward the bar, where Marco sat, hand wrapped around his glass and eyes focused on me too. I inhaled sharply and looked away, giving Chiara that *you did not just say that* look.

She giggled through her pearly-white teeth and wrapped the towel around her torso. "All I'm saying is that you could pull any guy in this room, and Alessa could barely pull Cristian for less than a year."

"As much as you don't want to believe it, Chiara," Alessa said behind us, walking up with her glass of wine, wearing a small blue bikini, "Cristian and I dated for far longer than a year. And your cute little friend *Roxie*"—she glanced over at me—"will be gone soon enough. Cristian might be slow in realizing how much of a pussy you are"—she pinched my cheek—"but I'm not."

Chiara smirked at her. "Think what you want, Alessa. Go try to win him back. I guarantee you that he wants nothing to do with you. He'd be downgrading from this"—Chiara gestured to me—"to"—Chiara looked Alessa up and down—"you."

"And if she's dead?" Alessa asked, smiling back. "He'll be sad, vulnerable Cristian, who comes running back to me for comfort, not to downgrade, you bitch."

As much as I wanted to do it, as much as I freaking dreamed of doing it, I couldn't seem to pull the gun out of my purse to kill her right then and there. Maybe I didn't want to make it public and draw attention to myself, or maybe I just wasn't ready to take someone's life. But, God, I wanted to do it so bad. I just … didn't have it in me to kill someone yet.

"Have a good rest of your night, girls. Enjoy it while it lasts."

She walked away from me and disappeared into the crowd, chatting with one of Cristian's many men and touching him like she hadn't just done the same to Cristian less than an hour ago. And what pissed me off even more was that Cristian didn't do shit about her. Whether she was his sister's best friend and his ex-girlfriend, he should've fucking kicked her off the boat the fucking moment she laid her nasty hands all over him.

48

roxie

"LOOKS like your face is healing from when Cristian kicked it in," I said to Marco, leaning against the bar in this tiny string bikini that Chiara had forced me to wear tonight, a drink in my hand.

She definitely knew how to capture the attention of everyone in the room, which I wasn't particularly fond of, but it helped me out when all eyes were on me and not Alessa—especially Cristian's.

Marco grabbed his drink from the bartender, swished it around, and didn't look in my direction because I knew that if he did, he would probably get his face kicked in again.

"You want to get me killed, Roxie?" he asked, sipping from his glass.

My lips curled into a smirk, and I jumped up onto the stool beside him. He glanced over, watching my breasts bounce in the small bikini.

"No," I said honestly because I didn't want him to die.

In some odd way, he was actually useful to me—or at least, I figured he would be.

"It doesn't seem that way," he said, hand tightening around the glass.

I gazed over my shoulder to see Cristian chatting with some of his men but staring right at me, his hooded eyes dark and heavy. I smiled sweetly at him and turned around in the stool to lean my back against the bar.

"How do I make it difficult? All I want is to ask you some questions."

"You want to ask me questions or wave your tits in my face?"

"If I waved my tits in your face, you'd be dead by now," I said, crossing one leg over the other. My gaze flickered from Cristian to Marco as Marco glimpsed at me. "Now, I have more questions about Alessa, and I need you to answer them for me."

Marco looked around the room, then turned to me. "What is it? And make it quick. If he thinks we're talking about something else while you're dressed like this—"

"Like what?"

Marco's gaze flickered down my body, jaw tensing. "Like a whore."

"Like a whore or someone you wouldn't mind fucking again?"

Marco growled. "You're fucking insane."

I smiled sweetly at him. "So ... questions."

"Make them quick," Marco repeated. "I don't have time for these games."

"Where does she live?" I asked, leaning closer to him and sipping my drink.

Jaw tense, Marco drew his tongue across his teeth. "What do I get for telling you?"

"To live another day," I said with a smile, seeing Cristian place his hand on some guy's shoulder, as if to say, *See you later; I have a girlfriend I need to take care of.* When Marco didn't reply immediately, I leaned closer to him and tilted my head to the side slightly, drawing my finger up his forearm. "Or maybe you don't care ..."

Marco pushed me off him, swallowed hard, and tried—hard—to hide that bulge in his pants. "I'll tell you, but you have to promise not to flirt with me in front of him. He already wants to kill me."

"And behind his back?" I asked, knowing that I would *never* cross Cristian like that. But seeing Marco squirm because of me was … fun, to say the least. The control someone had over a guy just because they had a pair of tits was astounding. I leaned closer and sipped my drink. "I see the way you look at me."

Marco cut his eyes to me and scurried off his seat, his hand over his crotch so nobody could see him. "You're fucking crazy."

"Where does she live?"

"Three floors down from Cristian."

My hands balled into fists. "She lives in our apartment building?"

Marco grabbed his drink and hurried past me. "You didn't hear it from me."

49

roxie

BEFORE MARCO COULD RUSH out of here, I slid off my stool and caught his wrist. "I want more information."

"You don't get any—"

Cristian clamped his hand down on Marco's shoulder, and Marco tensed.

"Leave," Cristian said to him, his voice impeccably low and dangerous, while his brown—almost-black—eyes were fixed on me. Sea breeze blew strands of his thick black hair onto his forehead. "And tell everyone else to get the fuck out of here too."

"We were just talking," I said to Cristian, brow furrowed.

"I don't give a fuck what you were doing." Cristian turned his head toward Marco. "I said to leave," he said into his ear, then shoved him away and toward the exit. "Party is fucking over. Everyone, get out."

Placing their drinks down and gathering their belongings, everyone began departing the yacht.

Cristian placed a hand on either side of me and leaned closer. "You think you can walk around all night, dressed like this"—he looped a finger around my bikini and tugged on it so hard that I could feel it start to come undone in the back—"and not be punished for it?"

"I was just"—I swallowed hard, heart racing—"having fun?"

Cristian glided his tongue across his lower lip and paused, clenching his jaw. "Out, Alessa," he said through gritted teeth, trapping me between him and the bar and not looking back at Alessa, who snatched her purse from a table and stormed off the ship.

When everyone left, including the bartender, Cristian took the strings to my bikini and jerked them up and down, making my breasts bounce. "Having fun, bouncing your tits all across my yacht? Making all my men stare at you? Is that fun?"

Warmth pooling between my legs, I swallowed hard and smiled. "Maybe."

"You don't get to walk around like this on my yacht anymore tonight," he said.

"But ... everyone is gone. You're gonna make me—"

He undid my top and pulled the strings on my bottoms to undo those too, letting them both fall off me and onto the ground between us. "This is how you walk around here now." He cracked a small smirk. "Why don't you go take a dip?"

Eyes lighting up with excitement, I tried hard to suppress a smile and turned toward the direction of the pool. Not only was this my first time ever on a yacht, but it would also be my first time ever skinny-dipping on a yacht with Cristian.

Cristian snatched up a fistful of my hair and smacked my ass hard. "Get in there quick, before I lose all control and fuck you out here," he murmured into my ear, pressing his hard cock against my backside.

As soon as he let go of me, I skipped through the rooms until I made it to the pool on the upper deck, jumping in before anyone from a nearby yacht could see me completely nude. When I came up for air and pushed some wet hair from my face, Cristian walked to the edge, shirtless and undoing his pants.

"I've never skinny-dipped before," Cristian said, kicking off his shoes.

"First time for everything," I said to him, grabbing him by the wrist and pulling him into the pool with me once he had taken off all his clothes.

He sank under the water and emerged a few moments later, shaking out his wet hair, water running down his tattooed shoulders.

Before I could stop him, he wrapped an arm around my waist, turned me over, and pressed me against the edge of the pool, my breasts pinned to the pool lining. He drew his nose up the side of my neck, making me shiver, even in the heated water. I curled my toes and pushed my ass back, wanting him inside me already.

This entire night, I had wanted him to finally take me.

I had gotten way too horny from all the attention.

Cristian wrapped one hand around my hip, positioned himself at my entrance, and rammed into me, the water splashing around us and sloshing over the edge and onto the concrete. Groaning in my ear, he wrapped his free hand around mine on the concrete, our fingers intertwining, and continued pumping into me.

"You're so sexy, *principessa*," Cristian murmured against my ear.

I let out a soft moan and clenched around him, the pressure building higher.

"And you're mine," he said. "Nobody—*nobody*—else's. Tell me you know that."

"I'm yours," I whispered.

"*All mine.*"

Fingers paling against the concrete, I leaned my head back against his shoulder. "I'm yours, Cristian. All yours."

50

cristian

THE NEXT DAY, I left Roxie at the apartment. I'd asked her to come work with me, but she'd refused. So, I tripled the security on our floor and in the lobby of the building, so she wouldn't be able to escape, no matter how hard she tried.

Part of me didn't think she would, but I still needed to trust her. She had gotten too close to Marco last night, so close that I demanded everyone leave so I could fuck Roxie senseless in the pool. I'd made sure she knew who she belonged to now.

Me.

Only me.

Staring down at papers in my office about more family members linked to the child trafficking ring that the cops were hunting down, I blew out a deep breath. If the cops found them first, the system wouldn't give the victims justice. I would because I'd kick their fucking heads in. The police would just throw them in prison.

By the sound of Charlie's screams, I'd say seemingly endless torture was worse.

My phone buzzed on my desk, and I reached for it faster than I ever had, hoping it was Roxie. I sighed when Chiara's name popped up on the screen along with a few short messages about the family.

Chiara: Alessandro found more names. One linked to Roxie.

Chiara: Underage vids. Roxie might be ... well, you know. I don't know how old the videos are, but Alessandro has been talking with Charlie for a while for any info.

Chiara: Meet me at 8 p.m. Our usual. Don't mention this to Roxie. I don't want her to freak out. She's already stressing over you.

Balling my hands into fists, I swallowed hard. My grandfather had killed Roxie's grandfather, but he hadn't eliminated the problem in our family—or hers either. I should've already done it. I should've known that there was more Roxie had been through.

"Have you seen my phone?" Marco asked, walking into my office and looking around, as if he had dropped it in here earlier this morning. But he hadn't been in this office for fuck knew how long.

I didn't want him in here or close to Roxie anymore. And last night, at the party, he had gotten too fucking close to her.

Kept staring at her.

And I fucking got it—Roxie was hot. But she was mine now.

I ran my tongue across my teeth and tightened my hands into fists under the desk, club music thumping through the thick walls. "Maybe you lost it last night when you were ogling my girl. Did it fall out of your hands while she was in the pool?"

Marco cut his eyes to me. "I wasn't looking at her."

Before I could stop myself, I shot up, grabbed him by the collar, and shoved him up against the wall, my jaw twitching in anger. "You're fucking lying to me now, Marco. I keep giving you the benefit of the fucking doubt. You lie because you want her."

Gritting his teeth together, Marco stared back at me and tried—hard—not to blow up in my face, but I could tell that if I pushed him more, he would break, and I would have another excuse to kill him right here, right now. I just didn't want that excuse to be my jealousy. Not after what had happened to my parents.

"Of course I like her," Marco said, tensing. "She's hot, feisty, *tight.* Is that what you want me to tell you, Cristian? I've been trying my best to avoid her, but she keeps coming back to me to piss you off. I'm not asking her to."

After glaring at him for another moment, I knocked him into the wall and released him, my hand aching—*aching*—to reach for my gun in my waistband and kill him dead. I had wanted to do it from the moment I saw the way she looked at him with all that excitement in her eyes.

Betrayal was fucking deep.

If I couldn't trust Marco, I couldn't lead this family.

I'd become just like my father.

"Get the fuck out of my office," I said, forcing myself to sit before I did something that I'd regret. "I have work to do, Charlie to deal with, and people to kill. And you don't want one of those people to be you."

Marco flared his nostrils. "That's it? That's all you have to say to me? Because keeping this shit about your father—about everything going on—bottled in, Cristian, is going to make you look weak and vulnerable to everyone else in this family, and you know what happened last ti—"

"OUT," I shouted at him, fury rushing through my veins. "NOW."

With that, Marco stormed out of the room and slammed my office door behind him, disappearing into the packed club. I didn't have the fucking time or patience to see his face anymore tonight. If I did, I would be weak, and I would kill him.

51

roxie

AFTER I'D BEEN HIDING in the hallway three floors down from Cristian's apartment for hours, Alessa finally walked out of an apartment and typed a code into her door to lock it. Dressed in a little skirt, probably out to slut it up with Cristian's sister, she tossed her hair over her shoulder and walked to the elevator.

I was here for information.

I waited for her to descend on the elevator, eyed her apartment door, and burned the room number four into my memory forever. I hurried down the hundreds of stairs to the lobby and was about to sneak out the front doors when I saw two guards standing directly in front of them and blocking my way.

Grumbling to myself, I walked up to one and pleaded with him to take me to the flower shop just across the street to buy some flowers to *spruce up Cristian's apartment*. It wasn't what I was planning to do at all, but he didn't need to know that.

Once I bought a dozen red roses, I scurried back into the apartment building and rode the elevator up to Alessa's floor. I pulled out Marco's phone and typed in his passcode—4576—which I'd seen him do about a hundred times now. I might've stolen his phone last night at the party because I needed to contact Alessa without her thinking anything of it. See, Marco *was* useful.

Me: Cristian has a surprise for you. He wants me to drop it off.

Within a moment, Alessa texted back.

Alessa: He does???

Me: Doesn't want you to know about it, so don't mention it to him if you see it today. But I lost your room code.

Alessa: 87346

I curled my lips into a smirk and typed her passcode into her door, pushing it open and stepping into her stupid fucking apartment. A wave of adrenaline rushed through me at the thought of breaking into and entering someone's home. It was illegal, but so was killing people, and this family had no problem with that.

And, come on, Cristian couldn't expect me to sit around all day.

I had nothing to do, no work to attend anymore, and had been trapped in by all these damn guards. I had to keep myself preoccupied somehow. Breaking into Alessa's apartment to find all the fucking dirt on her that I could was definitely a good way to keep myself busy without getting into any real trouble with Cristian.

Nobody would know.

Before anyone could see me, I shut the door and turned on the light. On the surface, this probably seemed like a terrible fucking idea—sneaking into your rival's home, telling her that your boyfriend wanted to give her a surprise, knowing that she'd kill you if she found you snooping through her stuff.

But to me, Crazy Roxie, this sounded like a wonderful idea because it killed two birds with one stone. I could find more information about Alessa, and when she asked Cristian later about the flowers "he" had left her—because that bitch wouldn't be able to help herself—it would prove to me if he was still into her or not. Because back at the yacht last night, he hadn't pushed her away.

And I fucking loathed that.

After snooping around for almost twenty minutes, I found at

least ten guns in her apartment, which I took all the bullets out of and tossed into the trash, a locked tablet, and a box full of pictures of Cristian and Alessa together and kissing, which must've been from months ago.

Nevertheless, it still fucking hurt.

They both looked so happy on the beach, a perfect couple who seemingly had no problems. A blonde beauty and a Mafia boss, who would rip your head off if you got on his bad side. And I couldn't help but feel a bit self-conscious because I looked nothing like her. If Cristian and I took pictures like this on the beach, I'd look like some kind of emo cow with tattoos covering my arms and a stomach that wasn't particularly flat. Not like a damn supermodel.

I blew out a deep breath and promised myself that I would never look at them again, but then I shoved them into my purse. I didn't know why I had done it. Maybe I didn't want Alessa to fawn over the pictures anymore, or maybe I just wanted to be angry with Cristian for ever dating someone as psychotic as her.

Continuing into her bedroom, I pulled out a notebook from her bedside drawer that had pictures of Cristian with girls throughout the years. There must've been twelve of them since he had just been a teenager, and each one had a red X over their faces. Except the last picture, which was a picture of me alone. Cristian and I didn't have any pictures together yet.

My eyes widened slightly, and I snapped the book shut. Alessa was fucking insane.

After deciding to leave as soon as humanly possible, I walked out onto her balcony, snipped a couple of flowers from the back of her balcony garden, and left them with a note on her table. I'd bet that she was too stupid to even recognize the flowers that she grew herself.

Hope you enjoy these. xx

I purposely didn't leave the roses that I bought because when Alessa thanked Cristian for them, Cristian would find out that, a few hours earlier, *I* had bought roses from across the street. And I didn't want word to get out to Alessa that I left them instead of Cristian. It had been my original plan, but this was easier and would confuse that stupid asshole.

So, I slipped out of her room with them and walked back to our apartment with those pictures in my purse and a nagging feeling in the pit of my stomach. I had thought that Alessa was all talk about killing me, but apparently, she had done it many, many times before.

52

cristian

SITTING in the car with Chiara, I stared out at the river and blew out a deep breath. "You're fucking kidding me, right? Please fucking tell me that you're lying and that this is one big fucking joke, Chiara, because I can't fucking do this right now."

Chiara frowned at the river, moonlight reflecting off her dark eyes. "Alessandro told me about it. He had been looking into it during your yacht party the other night. I'm sorry, Cristian. I saw the video and …" She paused, tears welling up in her eyes. "I can't believe that our families have ever done something like that … *to children.*"

"Fuck!" I balled my hands into fists and slammed one into the steering wheel. "Fuck. Fuck. Fuck. Fuck. Fuck." I ran my hand through my hair, my knuckles swelling slightly. "Let me see the fucking video. I need to see if it's her. I remember exactly what she looked like at that age."

Instead of pulling out her phone to show me, Chiara shook her head and pressed her trembling lips together. "It's her, Cristian. You don't need to see it. It's too bad. I'm afraid that you'll do something stupid."

"Do something stupid? Like fucking kill all those motherfuckers?" I snapped, glaring at her. "That's what they all fucking deserve. Roxie's entire family, every last fucking one who knew what was going on behind closed doors and didn't do shit about it. Now, give me your fucking phone."

After staring at me for a couple more moments, Chiara cursed under her breath, pulled her phone out of her pocket, and scrolled through Alessandro's messages until she reached a video. "We can't tell who the person behind the camera is, but you can hear his voice." With a shaky hand, she gave me the phone.

I snatched it from her and clicked play, my stomach in knots. Truthfully, I didn't want to see the video of my girlfriend getting molested by a man who was already dead, but, fuck, I needed to find out who was behind all this because these motherfuckers needed to be taken down now.

When the video started playing, I pressed my lips together and bit back a fucking sob. A sob from me—Cristian Ricci, the Manhattan devil—because nobody should ever have to experience something like that and have so much fucking trauma from it that they couldn't even remember it happening.

"It's either her father or grandfather," I said, closing the video after only a few moments. "And her older brother too. I heard him in the background. Where the fuck do they live now? Does Roxie still see them? Has she said anything to you about their whereabouts?"

Chiara shook her head. "She hasn't told me anything, Cristian. You told me yourself that she doesn't remember, but she never talks about her family that much. Has she said anything to you?"

Curling my hand around the steering wheel, I cursed under my breath. "No. She never talks about her family, never calls her family, not even when I first took her. I'm glad that she hasn't, but, fuck, what the hell am I going to tell her? I have to kill her entire fucking family now."

"For good reason," Chiara reassured, gently rubbing my shoulder. "She won't hate you."

But I wasn't sure about that. It took her so long—so fucking long—to even show the slightest bit of interest in me after I killed her fiancé. If I killed her parents too …

It needed to be done, but I didn't want Roxie to get hurt. Though either way, she would.

"I was going to suggest that you don't tell Roxie about it, but I think you should," Chiara said, letting me go and staring back out at the river, watching the water ripple. "This involves her, and if you really want her to be part of this family and for people like Alessa to respect her, she needs to be involved in what directly relates to her."

I ran my hand over my face and let out a silent groan, not wanting to mention this to Roxie, but knowing that I had to. I'd hated seeing how broken she looked after she found out what her grandfather had done to her. I wanted to keep this in to protect Roxie in every way that I could. I had told her that I wanted to make her Manhattan's most heartless killer, but … fuck.

Fuck.

"Fuck."

"I know," Chiara agreed. "It fucking sucks."

"I'll tell her, just not tonight."

Chiara cut her gaze to me. "Does that mean you're not really going to tell her?"

"I will, Chiara. I just don't know how she'll react. She's been … more aggressive than usual lately. I don't know if she's going to break down in tears or want to kill her family herself. If it's the latter, I need to make sure she's ready."

She laughed. "First off, I don't think Roxie will *ever* want to kill anyone, except your ex, Alessa, who keeps fucking with her, but that's beside the point. And, second, have you taken her to the range lately? She can shoot one bullet right through the center target. She's been practicing."

"She has?"

"Maybe if you keep pushing Roxie, she will kill Alessa for you."

My phone buzzed, Alessa's name popping up on the screen.

Alessa: Can't wait to see you. xx I'll be waiting at the apartment.

What the fuck was that about? I wanted to text her back and tell her not to go there because I knew that Roxie was trapped there tonight, but I thought it would be best if I headed there, so I didn't need to have Marco protect Roxie for me. That was my job, and Marco was already too close.

My stomach tightened, and my jaw clenched at the text. "I haven't been pushing Roxie."

Chiara rolled her eyes. "Not even at the yacht party? When you kept talking to Alessa throughout the night? When you should've been with Roxie, keeping all your men's prying eyes off her? Why'd you even invite Alessa to the party, Cristian?"

"This sounds like an interrogation," I said through clenched teeth.

"Roxie's my friend. I don't want an asshole like you hurting her even if you think you're doing something right. So, why'd you invite her?"

"I didn't invite her. My sister did."

"It's your yacht. You have final say on who is invited." Chiara turned toward me and tilted her head slightly to the side. "If you're fine with making Roxie jealous and trying to get her to snap that way, why don't you let Marco flirt with her a bit more? I think that's only fair."

I growled. "Get out of my fucking car."

Chiara smiled. "I'm just saying. You *do* want to keep Roxie pleased, right?"

"Out."

After laughing, Chiara opened the door and smiled at me. "See you later, and let me know what you want to do about Roxie's family. Alessandro and I will help in any way that we can. And be careful, Cristian. If you keep pushing Roxie, she will snap and kill Alessa."

53

roxie

AFTER WEASELING my way back into the apartment, I put the roses in a vase and placed them on the dining room table, feeling nothing but nerves about what I had just done. Sneaking into Alessa's apartment, taking all her bullets out of her guns, and even finding out about all those women she had killed before. She wouldn't get a fucking chance to do it again because I'd be ready for when she came next time.

Once I locked and dead-bolted the door, I placed the pictures on the counter and paced around the apartment, my heart racing faster than it should have been. And suddenly, I regretted everything that I had just done. If Alessa found out about it, she'd fucking kill me, and it wouldn't be a threat this time.

I would have a permanent home six feet under the ground.

Running my hands through my hair, I shook my head and thought about heading back to her apartment and taking everything back—the flowers and the note. It was stupid—so fucking stupid. And I was so terrified of what was going to happen next. I hadn't thought this through much because, truthfully, I hadn't thought I'd get this far.

Someone knocked on the door, and my mouth dried. I'd fucking known that Alessa would be over, but I hadn't expected it to be so soon. I thought that at least Cristian would be here, but ... he wasn't, and I was deep into a fucking anxiety attack.

I shouldn't have snuck into her apartment. I shouldn't have left those flowers. And I really shouldn't have written that note to her. I didn't know what I had been thinking at the time, but I hadn't been thinking straight. I have been blinded with revenge, desperate for answers.

Now that I had them, I wished that I hadn't.

Because Alessa had killed those girls, all of them, any who had seemed to just show minor interest in Cristian. Hell, I was full-blown *dating* him and couldn't get my mind around him not having done *anything* to stop Alessa yet. He should've killed her or thrown her out of the apartment building. He could have that arranged at the very least, couldn't he?

Alessa knocked again. "Roxie, open up. I know you're in there."

Heart fucking pounding, I ran through the apartment to find my gun. After making sure that it had enough bullets to at least protect myself from her, I walked back to the door and took a deep breath. I wanted so desperately to end this now. I didn't want to drag this on and live in fear anymore.

If Cristian wouldn't take care of her, then I would have to.

But could I?

I'd had so many chances and opportunities. Could I do it now?

Honestly, I didn't know if I could answer that question.

After cursing myself out, I stuffed my gun into my waistband—still holding it behind my back—and opened the door to see Alessa's *lovely* face smirking at me. Without permission, she walked into the room and kicked the door closed behind her, stalking closer and closer and closer to me. My hands wrapped around the gun's grip, yet I couldn't pull it out and end her. I couldn't.

My fingers trembled, my heart racing. How could I just end someone's life? How could *anyone* just end someone's life? I ... I ... I didn't know how Cristian or Alessa walked around without a fucking care in the world about it. Maybe they were both too fucked up and *should* end up together.

"Roxie," Alessa purred, heels clicking on the ground the closer she walked toward me, puckering her red-stained lips. "I *hate* to break this to you, but Cristian wants you out. He sent me flowers today and left me a cute little note that said he wanted me back." She stopped right in front of me and leaned in closer. "So, go pack your things and *leave*. I'll take back all the threats I've made to you and give you a chance to live your pathetic life again."

I swallowed hard, breath hitched. Nothing was that easy with her.

A moment passed, and she smirked.

"On second thought …" she started.

Before I had time, she pulled her gun out of her waistband, pressed it against my abdomen, and pulled the fucking trigger, the gun clicking, but no bullet coming out of it.

Alessa paused, her eyes widening, and pulled the trigger again.

Nothing.

I had taken all the bullets out of her gun when I snuck into her house.

But I wasn't going to let her go. I was going to kill her this time. I pulled my gun out of my waistband and pointed it at her head with a trembling hand.

"No more of your games," I said to her. "No fucking more of this shit. I sent those flowers, and I found how many people you'd killed. You're not going to end anyone else's life, especially not mine."

54

cristian

"HOW MUCH LONGER?" I said to myself through clenched teeth, needing to get back to the apartment building as soon as possible, but New York City traffic was fucking atrocious tonight, cars lined up for miles and headlights glaring in through the back windshield.

Laying on the horn, I sat back and cursed that I hadn't left Chiara sooner. I should've left Roxie in the house just outside the city today. But it was easier for me to sleep in my high-rise instead of heading back forty minutes each morning and night.

After concluding that I wouldn't be able to get back before Alessa could head up to my place with Roxie, I balled my hands into fists and called the head of security in the building.

The phone rang for a few moments, and then he answered, "Boss."

"Make sure that Alessa stays away from Roxie. I don't want them socializing."

"I'll get someone on it."

Once I ended the call, I pulled up Roxie's contact, something inside of me screaming to text her to make sure that she was okay because I knew how fucking crazy Alessa was. When we had been together, she'd threaten to end someone's life just for looking at me. I couldn't fucking imagine what she'd do to Roxie.

I should've thrown her out of the building sooner. I should've, but I hadn't.

Before Roxie had told me that she wanted me, I'd thought that she'd never ever think about me the way I thought and felt about her. I didn't think I'd actually get this far with her and have her love me back too. Part of me had always used Alessa to fall back on whenever things didn't work out with anyone else.

Now, I was going to fucking pay for it.

Me: Where are you?

No response.

Me: Stay away from Alessa.

No response.

Me: Fucking answer me, Roxie.

A few moments later, Roxie messaged me back, her response not sassy, like it usually was, which made me nervous. Roxie always had a sassy comeback, a remark that made me hot with anger, and I fucking loved it. Now … nothing like that.

Roxie: How many people has Alessa killed for you?

Instead of messaging her back, I dialed her number and waited for her to answer.

"Roxie," I said when she finally answered, my heart racing.

Alessa kept things on the down-low even if it had to do with me. It was how this family worked. Nobody spoke about killing someone else—we just did it. It kept cops out of our hair.

"How the fuck did you find out that she's killed anyone?"

"How many women, Cristian? And were you even going to tell me?"

"I don't keep track of who she kills, Roxie. Just stay away from her."

"How do you not fucking know?" Roxie asked me, voice harsh. "These women were your ex-girlfriends or flings or something to you. They just disappear, and you don't ask any questions about it?"

"I don't keep up with my ex-girlfriends."

"But you keep up with Alessa," Roxie said quietly. "You let her stay in your apartment building. You let her come to your parties. You haven't done anything about her, even when you say that you want to be with me."

My hand tightened on the steering wheel. "She's my sister's best friend."

"I don't care what she is to your sister. She is *your* ex-girlfriend, and she's threatened *me* one too many times now. You should fucking care, Cristian. I knew that you fucking killed people and tortured them, but I didn't fucking ask for this and for her to constantly show up around you."

I slammed my fist into the steering wheel. "She's threatened you? Why didn't you tell me about this sooner, Roxie? I would've taken care of her."

"I shouldn't have to tell you to take care of your ex-girlfriend. She shouldn't even be around you, and you fucking let her! I don't fucking understand you, Cristian. I fucking don't. I thought I could hold out a little longer, brush this aside, pretend like everything was fine, and ... and ... fucking do this, but I can't. She's killed so many girls, Cristian, and I refuse to be another one of them."

"How do you know about who she's killed?" I asked, trying to calm her down because she sounded like she was having a damn panic attack, like she had the night that I told her what her grandfather had done to her.

"Because she snuck into my apartment," someone said in the background.

My heart stopped, everything slowing down.

"Roxie," I whispered, my voice hoarse. "Roxie, please don't tell me that she's there with you. Please tell me that you're alone, that you locked the apartment door. Fucking please."

"You should've killed her when you had the chance, Cristian," Roxie whispered. "You should've done it for me."

"Alessa, I swear to God, if you fucking touch her, I'll end you for fucking good this time!" I shouted through the phone, chest tightening until I could barely fucking breathe.

If Roxie died, I didn't know how the fuck I'd be able to do this anymore. Everything I did was for her, since we had been kids. I'd waited so long. I should've been more cautious. But I hadn't.

This was my fault. My fucking fault.

The phone sounded like it clattered against the ground, then a gunshot rang out, the sound sending chills down my spine, and then the line went dead. I slammed on my brakes, my hands shaking and tears—fucking tears—welling up in my eyes.

I would end Alessa. I would kill her.

55

cristian

SQUEALING into the underground parking lot, I shut the car off and sprinted up the stairs to the lobby, not willing to even take the elevator yet. I needed to find out what the fuck was happening and needed to see where Roxie and Alessa were because I had told my security to watch them both.

And they obviously couldn't do that.

"Where the fuck are they?" I sneered at my guards in the lobby, heart racing.

"Boss," one started.

I grabbed him by the neck and thrust him against the wall. "Where the fuck are they?!"

He swallowed hard and pointed to the elevators. "Top floor."

After pushing him away, I slammed my fingers onto the elevator button and waited not so patiently for the doors to open. I wanted to run up the stairs and forgo the elevator altogether, but it would take longer. There were forty damn flights at least.

Once the doors opened, I paced around the tiny room and ran my hands through my hair, fury rushing through every one of my veins. When I saw that bitch's face, I was going to fucking torture the living shit out of her. Alessa had taken what was *mine*, what I had worked endlessly to find and have again.

She had fucking taken Roxie from me.

And she would pay with her blood and her life.

When the doors to the top floor opened, I stormed out and headed to my front door. Marco hurried down the hallway toward me with his brow furrowed and a concerned expression on his face.

"Cristian," Marco said, grabbing me by the arm and tugging back. "You don't want to go in there. You—"

But I could think of nothing, except killing Alessa. She'd fucking touched my girl, threatening her, and Roxie hadn't fucking told me about it. But I should've known. I should've been keeping better tabs on Alessa, and I certainly should've killed her by now.

All this time, I'd kept telling myself that I had been keeping her around because she was my sister's best friend. But the truth was that I was afraid to live this life alone. I was afraid that I'd grow old with nobody to ever truly love me, with Roxie hating me for eternity. And I knew that Alessa would die for me if I asked her to. It was never love with her, but at least it wasn't loneliness.

Though I didn't give a fuck now about spending life alone.

I'd rather spend it alone than with a bitch like Alessa.

Shoving my door open, I stopped dead in my tracks and sucked in a sharp breath. Blood had pooled in a puddle in the center of my foyer, staining the white marble tiles. I shut the door behind me, my fingers trembling. There was so much of it. Roxie had to be fucking dead, all because I hadn't done anything to stop Alessa.

A thick trail of blood led to the bedroom. With fear rushing through me, I followed it down the hallway and squeezed my eyes closed, not sure if I had it fucking in me to see Roxie in our room, dead. I would lose it—fucking lose it.

Pushing fear aside, I opened the door to see a woman lying in the bed on her stomach with blood soaked through her hair. Blinded with tears, I hurried over to her, turned her onto her back, and backed away with wide eyes.

It wasn't Roxie, but Alessa.

A bullet between her eyes, her carcass in my bed.

Before I could react, someone pressed the muzzle of a gun to the back of my head. "You got what you wanted, Cristian. You turned me into a monster—a fucking monster who kills people—all because you couldn't take care of your ex-girlfriend."

My breath caught in my throat. "Roxie."

When I went to turn around, she pressed the muzzle harder against my head. "Don't fucking move unless I tell you to."

Yet, still, I couldn't stop myself from turning to the side to see her face. I was so fucking relieved that Roxie was the one who had killed Alessa and not the other way around. I needed to see her, to hold her, to show her that I was sorry that I hadn't taken care of Alessa beforehand.

But when I turned fully, Roxie slammed a kitchen knife into my thigh, pain shooting through me and warm blood running down my leg.

She pulled it out and pushed the gun further against my head with a shaky hand. "Sit down on the bed, Cristian, next to your ex-girlfriend, before I have to kill you tonight too."

56

roxie

"DO AS I FUCKING SAY, CRISTIAN," I said through clenched teeth, warning him one last time before I accidentally did something that I'd regret. As hard as I tried, I couldn't stop the adrenaline pumping through my veins and my thoughts from running a million miles an hour.

Killing Alessa had been the most gratifying feeling in the world. It scared me how good I'd felt to watch the life drain out of her eyes and to know that her heart had slowly stopped beating because of me. She had made my life a living hell for the past few weeks and killed countless other girls for no good reason, all because they had once crushed on Cristian.

Cristian slowly sat on the bed, shoulders slumping forward while he yanked the knife out of his thigh. "Put the gun down, Roxie."

"No," I snapped. "You wanted me this way since the moment you laid eyes on me. You're not getting rid of me that easily. This is who you fucking made me out to be, so you'd better shut your mouth and enjoy it."

The words seemed to tumble right out of my mouth, and I

couldn't for the life of me stop myself from seizing control of the conversation and demanding my answers. This man had made me kill her and made me a murderer. This was what he got.

With the gun still pointed at him, I grabbed the box of Alessa's shit and placed it on the bed in front of him. He glanced down at it, then down the barrel of the gun and right at me, as if he wasn't scared that I could pull the trigger at any moment and kill him.

"What's this?"

"The girls your *girlfriend* killed."

Cristian clenched his jaw. "Don't call her that. She's not my fucking girlfriend."

I pressed the muzzle harder against his temple. "Open the box and look at it."

After cursing under his breath, Cristian opened the box and pulled out the pictures of the girls with red Xs over their faces. He laid them all out on the bed and stared at each one, brow furrowing and shaking his head.

"That could've fucking been *me* because you let Alessa stay in your life," I said.

"She wouldn't have done that to you."

"But you thought she did!" I shouted at him. "You thought she killed me! And she fucking tried to too." Nerves ran through my body, shooting up and down my arms and making them tingle. "Why, Cristian? Tell me why you let her stay so close to us. Tell me why you risked my life like that. You … you were supposed to fucking love me."

Cristian put all the images back into the box and placed it next to Alessa's dead body, then stood back up and postured over me. "Put the gun down."

Instead of letting him intimidate me, like he always did, I clicked off the safety and held my hands steady. "Tell. Me. Now," I said through gritted teeth, my patience running thin, yet I couldn't stop myself from feeling pain. "Do you still love her?"

Cristian didn't take another step toward me or even grab the gun. He just stared down at me with trembling eyes and gave a short shake of his head. "Don't be stupid. I could never love someone like her."

"Were you still sleeping with her?" I asked, desperate for answers.

Cristian curled his lips. "No."

"Then, why, Cristian?" My voice was quiet. I couldn't figure this fucking out, and I wasn't going to let him go because of it.

He had made me kill someone, and if someone caught me, I'd go straight to jail without Cristian's help.

I swallowed hard and looked him right in those dark, wavering eyes. "Do you not love me?"

"I don't fucking love myself sometimes, Roxie," Cristian said finally, breaking his gaze and staring at the empty space between us. He balled his hands into fists. "It's not because of you. You did nothing fucking wrong. I just didn't want to be alone."

My eyes widened. Anger. All I felt was anger.

"That's why you kept that bitch around?" I asked through clenched teeth, shoving the gun further against his forehead and making him tumble back onto the bed. "That's why you fucking kept her around out of all fucking people? Because you wanted to make sure that Cristian Ricci wasn't alone? What about after you killed my fiancé and took me? You weren't alone then. You should've dropped her, Cristian. You should've fucking done it!"

"I couldn't," Cristian said, voice shaky.

"Why not?" I asked, suddenly quiet again.

He opened his mouth to speak, but no words came out.

"Why couldn't you do it for me?"

"Because ..." he finally said, not making eye contact with me, almost as if he was ashamed. "I'm not a good guy, Roxie. You fucking know that. I don't fucking deserve you. I never have, and I was afraid that you would never love me. And the other night, when you finally told me that you wanted *me*, I ... feared that, one day, you'd wake up and see me for who I was and run off with Marco or leave me alone. My parents are dead, and my sister hates me. I don't want to be alone anymore."

He rubbed a hand across his face, licked his dry lips, and looked up at me. "I want to be with you, but you fucking deserve more than anything I could give you. You deserve to be happy and free of stress, not sitting around this apartment all day, worrying about when someone will try to kill you."

I paused for a long time and stared at the man in front of me, shaking my head and refusing to let him just push me to the side like that. He wasn't getting rid of me, not now and certainly not ever.

I trailed the muzzle against the side of his face and placed it right under his chin. "Prove it to me."

"Prove what to you?"

"Prove to me that you fucking want me, Cristian. Prove to me that you'll choose me over any other woman who was once in your life or who tries to be in your life. I see the way those girls at the club act around you. Show me that I will always be the one you come home to."

57

roxie

"PROVE IT TO YOU?" Cristian asked, the shakiness gone from his voice. He tugged me onto the bed with him, flipped me onto my back, and crawled between my legs.

My fingers relaxed against the gun's grip, and I nearly let it fall out of my hands, but he wrapped my fingers around it and pointed it right at his head.

"If you're going to point that gun at me, don't let it slip."

After gently pulling down my leggings and underwear, Cristian gazed down at my pussy, a smirk stretching across his lips. He brushed his fingers down the insides of my thighs, and I stayed completely still, feeling all the tingles and keeping my hands steady. He laid down on the bed on his stomach, his head between my legs, and held my thighs apart, pressing his lips to my pussy and thrusting a finger into me.

He massaged it in circles, each time a little faster, until I couldn't handle it any longer. I squirmed under his mouth and sucked in a deep breath, the pressure building already.

I stared down at him, breath caught in the back of my throat. "Tell me that only I am yours."

With those devilish brown eyes, he looked up at me. "Only you are mine."

He flicked his tongue against my swollen clit again, hitting me exactly where I needed him and making me moan out loud, pleasure rushing to my core. He pushed another finger into me and pumped in and out of me slowly.

"Nobody else will ever lie in this bed with me."

He flicked his tongue over and over against my clit, rubbing it in small, torturous circles and making me clench even harder. I squirmed under him, my hips moving from side to side as he continued to eat my pussy until I was about to come.

Just before I let out an unruly orgasm, he pulled away slightly and stared down at me with those devouring eyes. "You're going to come on me, *principessa*. You won't come on anyone else ever again —unless I give you permission."

My lips curled into a smile. "I'll come when I want." I pressed the muzzle harder against his temple. "You don't have control tonight, no matter how much you think you do, Cristian."

After he chuckled, I turned us over, so I straddled his waist and settled the muzzle of my gun right under his chin and against his throat, grinding my hips against his and making him harder. "Take off your pants and fuck me."

It wasn't a request, but an order.

Leaning back on one hand, he undid his buckle and zipper, pulled himself out of his pants, and rested the head of his cock against my entrance. I lowered myself onto him and blew out a deep breath, my body shuddering in pleasure. He seized my waist in his hands and slowly bucked his hips up and down, making sure to fill me with as much of his cock as he could.

Pussy clenching around him, I curled my toes and moaned. "Harder, Cristian."

Continuing to fuck my pussy, Cristian thrust into me and dug his fingers into my sides even harder. I clenched on him, knowing that I was so close and that, in a moment, I would come.

"Fuck it," I murmured, resting one hand on his shoulder and

bouncing up and down on his cock, the gun still aimed at his throat and my pussy becoming even tighter around him. "Don't move."

Cristian grabbed my ass in his hands, gently helping me move on him, and grunted. "Fuuuck, Roxie," he murmured into my ear, biting down on my shoulder and stilling completely underneath me. "Fuck, you feel so good."

Pleasure exploding through me, I collapsed onto him and tossed the gun down beside Alessa's body. Wave after wave of ecstasy rushed through me, and I blew out a deep breath, my mind all over the place.

Cristian wrapped his arms around my waist. I rested my head on his shoulder and kissed his neck.

"I love you, Cristian," I whispered to him. "And I'm not going anywhere."

58

cristian

"WHAT ARE you going to do with her body?" Roxie asked me, sipping on her Afterglow Elixir wine and remaining oddly calm for someone who had just killed a woman.

After I wrapped my thigh stab wound, we sat in the middle of one of Manhattan's most elegant restaurants, Roxie dressed in a satin red dress that hugged all those delicious curves.

Drawing a finger across the rim of her glass, she gnawed on the inside of her cheek. "Nobody will know what happened, will they?"

Trying to figure her out, I sat back in the seat. "It's already taken care of. Don't worry about it at all. You're under my protection, *principessa*. You're my girl now, and nobody will touch you for doing what you did."

"Not even your sister?"

My breath caught in my throat at the thought of facing her sometime soon. But either way, nobody was going to touch my Roxie. I had been through so fucking much for her. I wouldn't let my sister's wrath get in the way.

"Not even my sister."

Roxie slumped her shoulders forward, as if she had been waiting for me to reassure her about that for hours now, and finally relaxed in the seat. By the look on her face, I could tell she thought my sister would kill her for her killing her best friend. It had been a long fucking time coming, but I needed to sit down with my sister and finally talk to her about everything that had happened, especially about our parents.

"And Marco?" Roxie asked, glancing out the window to see one of the Ricci cars parked at the curb. Marco wasn't in it, but she didn't know that. Still, I couldn't decipher all that her expression held. "What happens to him?"

I sat back in my chair and sipped my drink. "What do you want to happen to him?"

Caught by surprise, she furrowed her brow. "You don't have a plan?"

"I do," I said to her. "But I want to know what you want me to do to him."

She gnawed on the inside of her lip. "I don't know."

"Then, I'll kill him."

Suddenly, she reached across the table and grabbed my wrist. "Don't kill him."

"He's touched you. Alessa touched me, and you took care of her."

"Because *you* couldn't," Roxie snapped, then pressed her plum-colored lips together and blew out a breath through her nose. "Sorry. It's just not his fault. It's mine. He told me to stay away from him, but I wanted to piss you off. He's not to blame, and he's only been good and loyal to you."

Wanting to keep Roxie on her toes, I smirked at her. "We'll see."

She widened her big brown eyes at me. "Cristian, please."

"Relax. I won't kill him. Not yet." I paused. "But there's something serious that I need to talk to you about. And ... you might want to finish that glass of wine before I tell you. You're probably going to fucking need it."

Instead of finishing the glass, Roxie pushed it away and leaned forward, worry etched onto every inch of her face. "Please, don't tell me there's another crazy woman who wants you. I don't know if I can deal with another."

My lips curled into a half-smile. "There is."

Roxie crossed her arms over her chest and looked at me with so much intensity that I thought she'd pull that gun right out of her purse and threaten me with it again, which did a little bit more than just turn me on. She had looked beyond sexy, pushing the muzzle against my temple and making all those cute deathly demands of hers.

Before she *could* kill me, I grinned wider. "And I'm looking right at her."

"Fuck you," Roxie said, letting out a breath. "You almost gave me a heart attack."

Taking her hands in mine, I dropped the smile and frowned. I didn't want to tell Roxie about her family. I really fucking didn't. It felt like one big thing after another, one big step backward after a small one forward. It was always something in this family.

"What is it?" Roxie asked, pulling her hands out of mine and pushing a strand of hair off my forehead.

"We found more people who have ties to child trafficking and … a video."

"A video? Of it happening?" Her lips formed a soft O. "That's terrible."

I swallowed hard, loathing this. "Yes, of it happening, and … your family is in it."

Roxie pulled herself away from me and stared at me with wavering brown eyes. "No," she whispered, shaking her head. "Please don't lie to me. Was my brother abused by my grandfather too? Did it happen to—"

"No. The video was of you when you were a child."

The emotion drained from her face, an unreadable expression crossing it. She stayed quiet for a moment too long, making me feel beyond uneasy. I should've kept my mouth shut, shouldn't have said anything. I could've easily taken care of this myself. But … this was the right thing to do. Roxie deserved to know and deserved to take action herself, if she wanted.

"I want to see the video."

I sat up and clenched my jaw. There was no way that I could let her see something like that. Last time, she'd had an anxiety attack in the middle of the hotel room and broken my damn heart with all those tears. If she saw a video of that actually happening to her, I feared something worse than that would happen.

"Roxie, you really don't," I assured. "It's not pretty."

After a few moments of silence, Roxie shook her head. "Nothing is pretty in this business, apparently, Cristian. I killed a woman today"—she lowered her voice and leaned forward—"put seven bullets right through her skull, and I don't feel any remorse. Let me see the video."

Though she hadn't shown one ounce of regret for killing Alessa —hell, I didn't either—I knew that, later on, she would feel something. Killing someone for the first time had really fucked me up, and Roxie might've been strong, but she hadn't been around this shit all her life.

"Roxie …"

"Now, Cristian."

Letting out a sigh, I pulled my phone from my pocket, scrolled to Chiara's messages, and found the video of Roxie being sexually abused that she had sent me after our meetup. It wasn't a pretty fucking sight, and I had wanted to delete it the damn moment that I saw it, but things had come up last night. Yet, still, I wished that I could refuse because it was sickening.

"I muted it for you. Don't turn it on. You're—"

Instead of listening to a word I'd said, Roxie turned the sound on the lowest damn setting and tapped the play button. The determination on her face faded quickly as she saw those terrible things happening for the first time in her life. While it wasn't happening to her now, she could really see and understand what had happened.

And the look of despair on her face told me everything I needed to know.

No matter the facade Roxie had put up this past night, she was hurting. Bad.

59

MY FAMILY.

My own family.

Not only had they all known about this, not only had they let it happen, not only had they encouraged it, but they had also recorded a fucking video of a helpless child and sent it out on the dark web for all the creeps and pedophiles to see.

I balled my hand into a fist under the table, my nails slicing into my palm, and held back a piercing scream.

Why the fuck would they have done that to me, their only daughter? How could my parents, my family, the only people who were supposed to love me, have done that to me? That was beyond fucked up.

Cristian went to pull the phone away, but I needed to see it all. So, I grabbed his wrist, pulled the phone out of his hand, and stared at it through tear-filled eyes. My lips trembled, blood seeped from my palm and onto my thigh. I couldn't think straight.

"Why did they do this to me?" I whispered once the video ended. "I was just a child."

After successfully pulling his phone away from me this time,

Cristian took another sip of his drink. "People are fucked up, Roxie. You're going to see some shitty things in this family. Shit you'd never imagine could happen does." He deposited his phone into his jacket pocket. "But I'm going to take care of this for you."

Unable to hold myself back, I shook my head. "No. I'm going to take care of this."

"You need to relax after what you did."

"No, I don't. This is my family, Cristian. This happened to *me*," I said through gritted teeth.

Rage pumped through my veins at the mere thought that this probably hadn't happened just once or twice and just to me. It probably happened dozens of times to dozens of kids. My family had ruined one too many lives, and I couldn't let it happen again.

All my life, my parents told me that the Ricci family had ruined their lives. Now, I knew why. The Ricci family might've been an organized crime family that laundered money, sold shipments of illegal drugs, and killed people, but they didn't stand for child trafficking or sex abuse. But my shitty family had.

I'd be the one to stop them this time.

I'd be the one to ruin their lives.

I'd be the Ricci that killed them all.

"This is going to sound crazy," I started, leaning across the table.

Hell, I felt fucking insane after tonight. Nothing felt real, everything so distant yet so close at the same time. I didn't understand it, but I wasn't going to back down now. I was in too deep, and I didn't want to come back out.

"What?" Cristian asked, brow furrowed.

"My family has always despised the Riccis, and I want to give them another reason to hate them." I swallowed hard, not sure how Cristian would take this and definitely not sure if this was the craziest thing I had ever asked or if it was just the wine talking in my ear. Either way, I grabbed his hands. "Me."

"You? You're not officially a Ricci yet."

"Not yet."

Cristian's intense gaze met mine, his breath catching in his throat. "You're fucking serious? Don't fuck around with me right now, Roxie. That's not funny because you know that I'll make sure you're mine *tonight*."

Butterflies fluttered around in my stomach at the mere thought of marrying Cristian *tonight*. Yeah, I knew that it was fucked up, but Cristian had said that he wanted to marry me, and I wasn't going anywhere now. I had a family to fuck over and a dead woman on my conscience. Why not pile on something else?

"Or ... I could always ask Marco to marry me. I'd be a Ricci then, right?"

Cristian yanked me forward, snaked his hand around my throat, and caught my bottom lip between his teeth. "Marco is not going to fucking touch you, *principessa*. You're mine. And if you want to be a Ricci, then you're going to be a fucking Ricci."

"Tonight?"

He stood, picked me up right out of my chair in the middle of the damn restaurant, and carried me out into the chilly NYC streets, pressing a fat, wet kiss on my lips.

"You'll be mine tonight, *Mrs. Ricci*."

60

roxie

"WE'RE GOING to have a real wedding one day," Cristian said to me. "Invite all the family, rent out a beautiful dining hall for the reception, get you a ring as big as your finger, and go on a fucking amazing honeymoon, but tonight, it'll be quick and intimate."

I walked into his high-rise, both shocked and excited that this was happening, and skipped with him to the bedroom. "I know we will. I've always wanted something big, but this is more important to me at the moment, just being with you."

"And taking my last name."

Rolling my eyes, I playfully shoved him back. "And taking your last name."

He grabbed my hand and pulled me farther into the room and to one of his dressers, opening it up and grasping a small box. A beautiful diamond ring sat inside it, sparkling under the room's dim light.

"It was my mother's. I was planning on getting you a new one, but that'll have to wait. I want to get you the most perfect one."

"This is beautiful," I whispered, drawing my finger against the stone.

Cristian pulled it out and slid it onto my finger, taking my hand and placing his lips on my knuckles. "You deserve more than this. You deserve a wedding with a family that'll always protect you, and you deserve to finally be happy."

My lips curled into a smile. "I am happy now."

He wrapped his arms around me and pulled me closer. "I vow to make you even happier, to kill anyone who tries to hurt you, and to get rid of all the women who bother you, like I should've done before. And…" He paused, a smirk crossing his face. "All your debts will be relieved once you have my last name."

I rolled my eyes and playfully slapped his chest. "As they should. That was the deal."

Suddenly, someone banged on the front door.

"Open up!" Chiara yelled.

After kissing Cristian, I took his hand and pulled him to the front door.

"What is going on?" Chiara asked, gripping Alessandro's hand and pulling him into Cristian's high-rise apartment in the center of the city. "You called me, like, five times and wouldn't tell me anything. What happened?" She wrinkled her nose. "And why does it smell like ten thousand liters of cleaning products were dumped in this living room?"

Cristian and I stood in the room, my hand intertwined with his.

I grinned at her and wiggled my brows. "Alessa is taken care of, and I—"

Before I could say another word, Chiara dropped her purse and placed her hand on her chest. "No, you didn't … oh my God, you did. You fucking killed that bitch. I told you she would, Cristian. I freaking told you. God, I'm so excited! That's why you look like a boss-ass bitch tonight!" She enveloped me in a hug. "You're officially part of the family."

"Actually, she'll officially be part of the family tonight."

"Tonight?" Chiara asked, brow furrowed.

As she pulled away, I held up my left hand and let her see the rock on my ring finger.

Chiara gasped and looked over her shoulder at Alessandro. "Step up your damn game. They've been together for a day, and they're already getting married. I'm waiting." Then, she turned back to me and pulled me closer again, jumping up and down. "I'm so fucking happy for you!"

"You're going to squeeze the woman to death, Chiara," Alessandro said. "Let up."

When Chiara pulled away, she grinned at me. "How long do we have? We have to get you all dolled up! We can slip you into that white dress you bought when we went shopping and make you glow like the fucking moon. This is your night, girl."

Cristian looked down at his phone. "Twenty minutes, and we can't be late."

"Twenty minutes it is," Chiara said, grabbing my hand and pulling me into the other room. After sitting me on the bed, she pulled out my makeup bag from one of the dressers and found the white dress in the closet. "You're going to be smoking hot."

She finished with three minutes to spare and pushed me in front of the mirror, her hands on my shoulders and a huge smile on her face. "Cristian had better give you a real wedding sometime in the coming months, but you'll remember tonight forever."

Yeah, I'd remember tonight forever—for a couple of different reasons. Learning what my parents had done to me definitely being one of them. Which made me remember that … I wanted to call them before this all went down. I thought congratulations was needed.

So, after ushering Chiara out to have a few moments of alone time, I picked up my phone. My stomach tightened in fear and anger as my fingers moved along the screen, dialing my parents' home phone. I hadn't talked to them in months, years maybe. We had never been close, and I liked to keep it that way, but now, it was fucking payback time.

Mom answered the phone on the third ring. "Roxanne, it's so nice to hear from you! I thought you'd changed your number. You never answer any of my calls." That was because she hadn't called. "The whole family is here. We're so excited to chat with you."

"Great," I said, my throat dry. "Can you put me on speaker? I have news."

After fumbling with the phone, Mom shouted, "Okay, sweetheart."

Before I could click off the phone and regret this whole thing, I blew out a deep breath and decided to just get it over with. "I'm getting married."

I paused to let them have a moment of happiness, just a moment of glee, that their only daughter had found someone to love her unconditionally.

When I heard the joyful chatter, I grinned. "Tonight, I'll be Cristian Ricci's wife."

All the chatter and whispering stopped, gasps echoing through the other side of the phone. My stomach tightened even more, this time in eagerness.

"Don't worry. We'll pay you a visit soon. We're both thrilled to see you."

61

cristian

"ROXIE! YOU READY?" I shouted, glancing down at my phone.

We weren't having anything big for the wedding, obviously, since this was last minute, but I had *friends* at the courthouse who could marry us in fifteen minutes. And I wanted to make Roxie my wife tonight. I had waited all my life to have her, and I wouldn't pass up this opportunity. She could change her mind by tomorrow.

Our bedroom door opened, and I stared at Roxie with wide eyes, my heart … racing.

"What happened to the white dress?" Chiara said when Roxie walked out of our bedroom, dressed in a black spaghetti-strapped sheer-mesh dress and a thick silver choker that sparkled under the living room light.

Roxie smiled at me. "I changed. White isn't really my color."

I grabbed her hand and twirled her around. "But black is."

"You're okay with me wearing this?" she asked with wide eyes.

Wrapping my arm around the small of her waist, I pulled her to me. "You look sexy."

"Enough with the cuteness!" Chiara said. "I'm getting jealous, and we're going to be late."

After I grabbed Roxie's hand, we hurried out of the apartment, down the elevator, and out into the good ol' New York City night. Since traffic was horrendous and the courthouse was only a few blocks down, I walked beside her toward our future.

It felt so surreal. Hell, all of this did.

Three blocks later, I urged Roxie up the front steps of the courthouse with a smile. A car skirted up to the side of the road, my sister parking in the midst of traffic and storming out of her car and toward us.

I looked over my shoulder at her, cursed, and told Roxie to go in. "I'll be there in a second."

Roxie looked at my sister, gnawed on the inside of her cheek, and nodded. "Okay."

After Chiara glanced between us, she and Alessandro followed Roxie into the building. I blew out a breath and turned on my heel, facing her for the first time since the yacht party. To say I had been avoiding her would be an understatement. I didn't want to hear her complain.

"What happened to Alessa?" she asked, hurrying up the steps.

"I don't know what you're talking about."

She stopped in front of me and crossed her arms over her chest, tapping a red-bottomed heel on the pavement. "Last time she texted me she said that she was going to see you. Where is she?"

"I have no idea," I said because, well, I didn't.

After Roxie had killed Alessa, my men had taken care of her body. She could be six feet in the ground, burned, or down in the river by now. I didn't know where she was, and I'd like to keep it that way because, knowing Alessa, her ghost would come and fucking haunt me.

"What happened to her?" my sister said. "I know that you know."

Deciding that she'd find out sooner or later, I pressed my lips together. "Roxie killed her."

My sister paused for a moment, and then ... she laughed. Straight-up *clutching her stomach, tears flowing down her rounded cheeks, smile almost too wide* laughed. "Good one. Very fucking funny, Cristian. Roxie wouldn't hurt a fucking bee." She wiped some tears from her cheeks and glanced back up at me. "Where'd Alessa go?"

"Roxie killed her," I repeated, sounding out each word for emphasis.

She shook her head. "I'm being serious. You can drop the act."

"What the fuck do you want me to say to you? Roxie unloaded seven bullets in her brain in my apartment. I'm surprised Roxie didn't blow Alessa's entire fucking head off her shoulders. You don't have to believe me, but your annoying-ass friend who wouldn't leave me alone isn't coming back."

My sister paused, the laughter dropping from her face. "You're being serious?" she asked, anger replacing her expression. She balled her hands into fists and gritted her teeth, glaring at the door that Roxie had disappeared behind moments ago. "She fucking killed my best friend?!"

Before she could barrel into the courthouse, I grabbed her hand and pulled her back. "Your best friend had killed all the women I had ever been with and had been threatening Roxie for weeks. She deserves to be dead, no matter what you think."

After a few moments of standing before me in complete shock, my sister shook her head. "What the fuck, Cristian?" She shoved me. "And why the fuck are you here with Roxie? What the hell is going on? You can't let her get away with this! She deserves to die for what she did, and I'm going to be the one who—"

Before she could finish the damn sentence, I slapped my hand across her mouth and dug my fingers into her cheeks until my fingertips turned white. "Don't you dare threaten to kill Roxie, or I'll kill you. Do you understand me? If anything happens to her, I will end you without a second thought."

My sister stared up at me with wide, fearful eyes.

I shoved her away from me and stepped back. "Now, if you'll excuse me, I'm going to go get married."

Walking up the rest of the stairs, I disappeared behind the doors and said hello to a couple of officers lingering in the lobby, who had been trying to take me down for years now. But they could never find any dirt on me.

One nodded to me. "You turning yourself in?"

"I'm getting married."

And with that, I walked down the hallway and found Roxie standing in front of a woman and a piece of paper.

She handed me a pen. "You sign it first," she said, cheeks a rosy red, and smiled.

I took it from her and signed my name on the line, handing it back to her and waiting for her to put her signature down to solidify our marriage. She took the pen back, looked me up and down, and signed her name, officially becoming *Mrs. Roxanne Ricci.*

62

roxie

"ROXIE RICCI," Cristian murmured into my ear, his hands all over my body before I could even open our front door.

He moved his lips down the column of my neck, sucking and biting on my skin and leaving blotchy red marks that would tell everyone I was his.

Once I finally steadied my hand enough to push the key into the lock, I shoved the door open and stumbled into the high-rise with Cristian behind me, unzipping my dress and pulling it off my body, my heels staying on for tonight. With all the straps, they had by far been the hardest thing to get on tonight, and I didn't need the hassle of trying to take them off while Cristian was fucking me.

He wrapped one hand around the front of my throat, the other over my mouth and nose, making it hard for me to breathe, pinning me against the kitchen counter and grinding his hard cock against my ass. "You're fucking mine, Mrs. Ricci. All fucking mine, no matter how much you beg, scream, or cry tonight."

Breath slowly leaving my lungs, I went to inhale, but he restricted my breathing even more. I arched my back, giving him what he wanted and grinding myself back against him, twerking my hips up and down across his bulge.

"Just like that, *principessa*."

Wanting to have some dark fun with him, I leaned over the counter and grabbed a knife from the knife block while his face was buried in the other side of my neck. When he whirled me around and pressed me against the counter, hiking one leg up and undoing his pants, I held the knife to his neck.

"Make it hurt tonight, Cristian. I want to feel good."

Eyes widening from the pressure against his neck, Cristian smirked at me. "You want to play with knives, *principessa*?" he asked me, pushing himself balls deep inside of me and filling me up with his huge cock.

Before I knew it, Cristian had taken the knife out of my hand and forced it against my neck, trailing it down my chest and hooking it under the strap of my push-up bra. "Be a good girl for me tonight, and I won't hurt you *that* bad."

Heat gathering in my core, I sucked in a breath when he cut my strap in two pieces with just the knife's edge. It fell, my breast weighing the cup down and making it shift just enough to show a bit more cleavage. Cristian trailed the blade across my collarbone, stopping right in the center and smirking at me.

I tightened around his cock, my pussy walls clinging to him.

He cut off the second strap and swept the knife between my breasts and along my bra line. "You're so tight for me," he said, starting to pump into me, each time making my breasts bounce and push further into the blade. "If I fucked you any harder, this pretty chest of yours might turn red with your blood." He paused and glanced at me. "But you said you wanted it to hurt."

Cristian thrust up hard into me, the knife pressing harder against my tits, and started to really pound up into me until I came out of the push-up bra completely. I moaned out and clutched the countertop, shoving my breasts forward because I loved this.

Too fucking much.

"Harder," I pleaded.

Cristian forced the edge harder against my sternum as he rammed himself into me. Wanting, needing, desperate for more, I did what I'd never thought I could or *would* do—I raised a hand and smacked him right in the face.

"I said, I want it harder."

Overcome with anger that I had slapped him, Cristian pulled himself out of me, turned me back over so my chest was against the counter, wrapped one hand around my throat, and pushed the blade against it with the other. He pushed himself back into me and fucked me over and over and over, his huge cock thrusting in and out of my tight hole.

My fingers dug into the countertop until they turned white. I gasped out for breath, moaning and clenching on him. "More. More. More. Please," I pleaded, knowing that he was about to tip me over the edge.

He pumped into me one last time, and I screamed out, my legs trembling and waves of pleasure rushing through every part of my body until I could barely stand.

Cristian tossed down the knife, wrapped his arm around my waist, and buried himself as deep as he could get, coming inside my pussy. "My wife."

63

roxie

CRISTIAN LAY IN OUR BED, eyes shut softly and a five o'clock shadow on his face, looking as if he wasn't the cruelest crime lord in New York City. I sat next to him with his phone in my hands and his messages with Chiara pulled up on the screen.

That video played over and over and over again without sound. And I couldn't get myself to stop watching it. Cristian had fallen asleep hours ago, but I had stayed up all night after we had sex because … I felt both betrayed and angry that my own family could do that to me.

No matter how many times I shut the phone off and placed it in my lap, vowing that had been the last time I would ever watch it, I would pick it back up and glare at the video, at the sight of little Roxie being abused and not knowing why this was happening.

I felt her pain every time she opened her mouth, knowing that she was screaming in horror, shouting, "It hurts. It hurts. Please, stop."

None of them had ever stopped.

It'd kept happening for years—until Cristian's dad killed my grandfather.

And then maybe in private after that.

I couldn't quite remember, and I didn't want to remember either. I hated my entire family, should've cut them off sooner. I hadn't talked to them in so long, but … that didn't mean I didn't think of them, that didn't mean that I had been blinded for all these years by the facade they put on in front of everyone else.

In the video, little Roxie cried tears, her cheeks flushed red and her pouty lips swollen. I bit my lip to hold back a cry. I hated my parents and family so fucking much. I couldn't wait to destroy their lives, just as they had destroyed mine. It wouldn't make me feel better, but it'd stop the abuse now. It would end it. No other child would get hurt because of them.

"Have you been watching this all night?" Cristian asked from beside me, grabbing the phone from my hand and clicking it off.

Letting him take it, I pressed my lips together and glanced down at him. "I want to go now. I can't wait another moment. They've hurt me so badly, and God only knows how many other children have suffered because of them."

Cristian deposited the phone in his bedside drawer, sat up, and drew me into his arms. "*Principessa* …" he murmured into my ear, stroking my hair and pressing his lips to my cheek. "Calm down. You shouldn't have watched that. Don't work yourself up again, like you did in Boston."

After balling my hands into fists, I stared at New York City's skyline through our high-rise windows, the lights dancing against the dark morning sky. It couldn't have been later than five a.m., but I wanted to go. Now.

"How could I not get worked up, Cristian? They've done terrible things."

"And they'll pay for it," Cristian said. "But don't go in there upset. They will have won that way. They'll know that they broke you down. You're stronger than that. Show them how strong you are. Prove to them that you should've never been fucked with. Then, give them what they deserve. You hold the power. Don't let them win."

Letting his words set in, I sighed and rested my head on his shoulder. When I had been younger, they had taken away all my control; they had forced me to do things that no child should ever have to endure. Now that I was out, they still controlled me because this pain wasn't going away easily. I would forever wonder why my family had done that.

But … I wasn't going to let this loom over my life anymore.

I was Roxie Ricci, wife to the most dangerous mob boss in NYC and a woman who was about to take back control of her past, present, and future. And nobody was going to stop me, not Mom, not Dad, not my brother, and certainly not my grandmother.

"Okay," I whispered, moving off of him and walking to the closet, where I had stored my gun after I murdered Alessa last night. I pulled it out of a drawer, checked to make sure it had enough bullets in it for each of my family members, and turned back to Cristian. "I'm ready."

Cristian lay against the headboard with a smirk on his face and his chest bare. "Fuck, Roxie. You're so fucking sexy with that gun in your hands." He stood up and walked over to me in all his naked glory. "Nobody could ever compare to you. Ever."

My lips twitched up into a smile, my heart racing. Part of me still couldn't believe that, all within a night, I had killed someone and become Cristian's wife, who he actually … adored. He had wanted me to be the villain, wanted to make me into something that I wasn't … but maybe, deep down, I had always been the girl who would do what it took to get what she wanted *and* needed.

I'd just needed a little push from him.

"Can we go?" I asked impatiently.

He chuckled, grasped my face to kiss me, and walked into the closet to grab some clothes. When he came back out, he counted the bullets in his gun, then shoved it into his waistband, twirling his keys on his other finger. "Anytime you want, *principessa*."

Taking his hand in mine, I walked with him to the front door, pulled him out into the hallway, and found myself heading toward the elevators and feeling like the baddest bitch to walk the face of this planet. It was stupid and probably hella fucking embarrassing, but I felt good—too good.

"Have your parents moved?" Cristian asked once we were on the road and heading toward the town that they lived in.

I said my goodbyes to the city, knowing that I'd return later as a new person, and gazed out the windshield. "No. They barely leave their small town. They're still there," I said, stomach tightening the closer we got to their house.

The forty-five-minute drive seemed to fly by. I clutched the gun in my hand until my knuckles turned white and bounced my knees up and down, unable to hold all my nerves inside of me, especially when Cristian pulled up into the driveway and *everyone*'s car was there—Mom's, Dad's, my brother's, and my grandma's.

For years, I'd wondered why they all lived together. Now, I understood.

"You ready?" Cristian asked once he parked the car.

But I was already out and storming up to the front door with the safety off my gun and insurmountable heartache from all the fucking pain I'd had to endure. I wasn't upset; I was furious, angry, and heated.

Slamming the side of my fist against the door, I swallowed hard. One moment passed, then two, and then I heard Dad call that he was coming to answer the door.

And when the door finally swung open, I pointed the gun at his head and pulled the trigger.

64

roxie

DAD SMACKED AGAINST THE GROUND, his skull cracking in two and blood gushing out from the hole in his head. Unable to stop myself, I pointed the gun at his groin and shot one more bullet into him because I had nothing but rage and fury left inside of me.

My own family had encouraged this.

The lights turned on in the hallway, Mom's footsteps pattering toward us almost at lightning speed. "Steve?" she called out, rounding the corner and stopping dead in her tracks when she saw me and Cristian standing inside the entryway with Dad in a puddle of blood.

"He's dead," I said lifelessly.

She screamed at the top of her lungs and rushed toward him, picking up his corpse in her arms and crying loudly, as if she wanted the neighbors to hear her. But they hadn't heard me screaming for help and for my family to stop. My parents had bought this house for that reason—it was secluded.

And now, it was biting them in the ass.

"How could you do this to your father?" Mom screamed at me, cheeks stained with tears.

She sobbed so ugly that I wanted to end her right here and right now, but I needed to know how she could let her daughter be abused, how she had fucking lived with herself for all these years, knowing how fucked up she had left me.

"He loved you," she snapped.

"That's why he let me go over to Grandpa's house and spend time alone with him in his garage?" I asked, voice stronger than I'd thought it would be. "You loved me so much that you let him do whatever the fuck he wanted to do with me." I gave an empty laugh. "But it was all out of love, right?"

Mom paled and set Dad back down. "Honey, I—"

I pointed the gun right at her and nodded toward the hallway. "Get Grandma and my brother. I'm going to show the three of you how much I love you guys back, how much I *appreciate* everything you did to me."

When Mom didn't move, I aimed the gun at her foot and shot it, purposefully missing by a couple of inches. She yelped and hurried down the hallway, calling for my grandma and my brother, slamming open doors, begging them to come see me.

I stepped into the hallway with Cristian behind me, his hand on my lower back, guiding me to the dining room. My hand tightened around the gun when I saw my brother run a hand through his hair and step out of his room, yawning.

When he saw me, he widened his eyes and held his hands up. "Roxie, what are you doing?"

"Shut up and sit down," I said through clenched teeth.

Holding his breath, he scurried to the dining room table. Mom walked back out, sliding against the curve of the wall to stay as far away from the gun as possible, and sat down next to my brother.

I glanced down the hall. "Where's Grandma?"

"Please," Mom begged with tears in her eyes. "Let her live the rest of her days in peace. She doesn't have that much longer to live. She got sick after you left. Just … please, she doesn't deserve it."

Not having it, I clenched my jaw. "Grandma! Get out of bed."

A moment later, she glanced out of the spare bedroom, hunched over and giving me a small smile. "What is it, dear?" she asked, grabbing the wall for support.

I hated seeing her so fragile and weak, but … I couldn't let this go on any longer. She had taken part in this too. Whatever I ended up doing to her, she fucking deserved it. She had taken away my childhood, and nobody could give it back.

"Get the fuck out here," I said through clenched teeth.

Grandma grabbed her cane and walked out into the hallway, slowly making her way to the dining room table. I held the gun steady by my side once she sat, wanting to end them all. Cristian told me to stay calm, but I couldn't. I fucking couldn't.

I turned to my brother first. "Did you touch me?"

"Roxie, what are you even saying?" he asked, turning this back on me, like they all did. "You're going to have to be more specific. I don't know what the fuck you're talking about. You're cra—"

Unable to stop myself, I shot him in the knee. "Did. You. Touch. Me?"

Crying out, he grabbed his knee. "They made me, Roxie. I—"

"They didn't make you. I saw the fucking video. They weren't forcing you to watch as Grandpa assaulted me. You did it because you wanted to!" I screamed at him, lifting the gun a couple of inches. "Admit it! Admit that you did it and don't regret it."

My brother stared at me, lips trembling, and said, "You're fucking insane, Roxie. Insa—"

I didn't let him finish. I shot him in the head.

Mom screamed as her only son collapsed on the table, blood seeping from his head. "Roxie! What are you doing? That was long ago, so long ago that none of us remember it. We're sorry that it happened. I should've stopped it."

"But you didn't," Cristian said from behind me.

She cut her gaze to him, a scowl on her face. "Shut up."

"Don't talk to my husband like that," I said to her.

"You're not serious, Roxie, are you?" she asked, fingers trembling. "You can't marry a Ricci. They have done terrible things to our family."

I stepped toward her. "Funny thing is … what they've done to us is *nothing* compared to what you have done to me and to God knows who else. The Riccis were cleaning things up while you were dirtying them. Grandpa got what he deserved."

Mom lunged at me—fully lunged in a fit of hatred—and I did what I had done to the rest of them. One bullet, right through her head, to end her pathetic life and her rage toward the goddamn world.

With one bullet left, I turned to Grandma, who sat at the dining table without looking shocked or scared.

She grabbed my hand with her wrinkled one and pulled the gun to her heart, eyes wavering. "I knew that you'd find out and come back. I did something bad. I stood by as your grandfather and family used you, Roxie. I should've been a better grandmother and protected you."

"Your apology doesn't change anything. You can't give me my life back."

"Dear …" she said, pushing a tear off my cheek. I hadn't even realized I had started crying. "I didn't intend for it to change what will happen. Your grandfather deserved this. Your father, your brother, and your mother deserved this. And so do I."

Another tear fell down my cheek, my throat closing.

"I have regretted my choices every single day, and I don't deserve to live any longer. End this now. Please. I've tried for so many years with planned falls, pills, everything. I just want it to end. End it, Roxie, please."

My fingers shook, tears streaming down my face.

I pulled the trigger.

I put a bullet right through her heart.

I killed her.

And … I didn't regret it.

"You didn't win," I said to the room of my murdered family, wiping the tears from my cheeks. "You might have thought that you did for a while, but you didn't. Whatever you started began and ended with me. I'm going to make sure that nobody else feels my pain."

65

roxie

OUTSIDE, Cristian called a couple of his men to come clean up my mess. They were to burn the bodies or dump them in the deepest depths of the ocean or throw them in the landfill, like the garbage they were. I didn't know what they were going to do with four dead people, but I wasn't going to ask. Cristian had done this hundreds of times before me. He knew what to do.

I walked into my old bedroom and closed the door behind me, the room eerily quiet and still neat, like I had left it years ago. Except the bedsheets, which were wrinkly in a few different spots. Walking over to the bed, I drew my fingers across the creases to smooth them out, only to see a picture of a young Roxie on the sheets and feel something crusty on the bedsheets.

Rage and disgust rushing through me, I grabbed the sheets in my bare fists and pulled them off the bed. Unable to stop myself, I ran around the room like a madwoman, knocking down tables and chairs and picture frames, throwing stuffed teddies and ceramic pots that I'd painted in sixth-grade art class against the walls.

Everything.

Every.

Fucking.

Thing.

It had all been violated in some way, shape, or form, my childhood ripped away and stolen from me. Nothing could ever be innocent, nothing okay. Everything of mine reminded me of them and what they had done to me, even after I was long gone.

After I punched holes in the walls until my fists bled, ripped off the wallpaper, and tore the room apart until no childish part of me was left, I collapsed onto the bed and let the tears race down my cheeks. I hated them so much—so fucking much.

I had come here for answers, but I'd just killed them instead.

Nothing felt better. I didn't feel better. I didn't know if I ever would.

This would forever be etched into my memory, would always be a sour taste on my tongue. I wouldn't smile and tell my kids that their grandma and grandpa loved them, about all the wonderful stories I had about them. No, my kids would get nothing from them. Their lies, betrayal, and heartbreak ended with me.

"Are you okay?" Cristian asked from the doorway.

I glanced up through teary eyes, wondering how long he had been watching me. Had he witnessed my whole tornado of a disaster, ripping apart everything that I'd once called home, everything I'd thought was safety and security?

"No," I whispered truthfully, "I'm not okay."

He walked into the room and sat on the edge of my bed, pulling me into his arms. I curled up into a ball and sobbed into his chest, hitting him to get my anger out because I knew he'd let me. It wasn't right; he hadn't done anything wrong, but ... I couldn't keep it in any longer.

"Why?" I screamed. "Why? Why? Why? That's all I keep asking myself."

"It's not your fault, *principessa*," Cristian said, placing a kiss on my forehead. "Don't blame yourself for them being sick pieces of shit. You did nothing wrong, and you wouldn't have been able to fix them if you'd tried."

But his words didn't make me feel any better. Even though he was a hundred percent right, I knew that I would blame myself for this for weeks, months, maybe even years to come. I couldn't fathom anything that had happened, didn't know if I ever could.

When I finally gathered enough strength to pull away from him, I wiped my wet eyes. "I want to stop this. I want to help you and Chiara in some way. We need to clean up the family and get rid of anyone who has ever done something like this."

Cristian picked me up and set me on my feet. "My girl."

After taking my hand, he pulled me down the hallway. As I walked through the house, I stepped in something wet, which smelled like … gas. When we reached the front door, Cristian pulled a match out of his pocket, lit it, and handed it to me.

"Do the honors. End this for good."

I grabbed the lit match from him, tossed it behind us, and walked away with him as flames engulfed my childhood home. This wasn't the end, like Cristian had said. This was just the beginning, and I planned to rain fire down upon all the people who had taken advantage of helpless children.

Start reading *Mafia Toy*, the next book in this series, now!

also by emilia rose

Contemporary Romance

about the author

Emilia Rose is a *USA Today* best-selling author of steamy romance. Highly inspired by her study abroad trip to Greece in 2019, Emilia loves to include Greek and Roman mythology in her writing. She graduated from the University of Pittsburgh with a degree in psychology and a minor in creative writing in 2020 and now writes novels as her day job.
With over 18 million combined book views online and a growing presence on reading apps, she hopes to inspire other young novelists with her tales of growth and imagination, so they go on to write the stories that need to be told.
Join Emilia's newsletter for exclusive giveaways, early chapter releases, and more!

scan the qr code with your phone to view all books by emilia rose